BAD BOYS DO IT *Better*

In Love With an Outlaw

A NOVEL BY

PORSCHA STERLING

Trouble.

Janelle

I was anxious. I was excited. I was nervous. I was probably about fifty different emotions all at the same time. And I'm not positive that's even scientifically possible, but if any world renown and brilliant scientist had ever said it was not so, I'd be the perfect case study to prove that wrong.

Today was my first day as an official attorney. Sure, I was fresh out of law school and had no real experience beyond what I'd learned in class but still, I was finally official. Sitting at the prosecutor's table with four other assistant district attorneys, I could barely stop wiggling in my seat. We'd been sworn in only that morning and then whisked away to witness the very last day of trial for the district attorney's case.

Mike Pelmington was a brilliant attorney, and I had heard stories about him all throughout my time in law school. To be able to work beside him was an honor. After years of working in corporate law and focusing on corporations who were taking advantage of their employees, he decided to adhere to the pleas of his city that was suffering from the increase of gun and drug violence, and took on criminal law.

In a matter of a year, he'd put away nearly every big-time arms dealer and drug kingpin in the city, and the crime rate had dropped significantly. What he didn't know is that by getting rid of the powers in charge, he helped to make way for one of the most dangerous and violent crews of them all: a group of brothers that reeked absolute havoc wherever their name was mentioned.

Finally, after months of trying to get at them, it seemed like he finally got a break in the case when the youngest of the Murray brothers, Luke 'Outlaw' Murray, was caught on video nearly beating a man to death with his gun. The only other person who had been present during the assault agreed to testify against Luke, something no one had ever considered, and that brings us back to me. This was *my* moment.

Well, *technically* it was District Attorney Pelmington's moment, but it was mine too because I was able to sit in on the last day of the trial that was supposed to be his biggest. With the testimony of the victim, it was a definite that there would be a guilty verdict on not only Luke Murray, but eventually his brothers too. And I was able to witness the whole thing.

Suddenly, a voice cut through my daydream of what was to come and I felt someone pat me gently on the arm. Clearing my throat, I turned and looked into a set of gentle brown eyes.

"I don't think I was able to introduce myself to you earlier. My name is Chris… Chris Harvaty. I'm from Omaha."

Chris held out his hand to greet me as I sized him up in a matter of seconds. He was attractive in a boyish kinda way. Definitely my type. He had smooth, caramel skin and beautiful light brown eyes. I'd noticed him right when I walked in to be sworn in that morning, but my nerves were too on edge to really look at him. Reaching out, I placed my hand in his and shook it, giving him a small smile.

"Nice to meet you. I'm Janelle Pickney… from Atlanta," I informed him, my voice barely above a whisper as I rushed the last part of my response out. He smiled back at me and I felt my stomach flip-flop. Then his eyes darkened as a thought passed through them right before they tugged downwards into a squint.

"Janelle Pickney… from Atlanta," he repeated slowly, his eyes running over my face as his thoughts ran through his brain.

Oh God, I thought as I watched him, my cheeks stinging with dread. *Here it goes.*

So one thing I should mention is that my father is George Jefferson Pickney. Yes, George Jefferson. My grandmother is a huge fan of *All in the Family* and *The Jeffersons*. But anyways, my father is kind of a big deal. Well, actually, he's a really big deal. He graduated from Yale Law at the top of his class and against all odds. My grandmother was wild in her day. And when I say 'wild', what I really mean is that she was a hoe. A really big hoe. She would flip men the same way people changed drawers and didn't really care who knew it. Eventually, she got mixed up with my grandfather who was nothing but trouble. He was abusive in all ways: mentally, physically, emotionally… just bad news.

After she got pregnant with my father, she tried to get her life together and left him, moving all the way from Las Vegas to Atlanta only a few months after she learned she was pregnant. She was poor and didn't have a dollar to her name, but she did everything she could to survive. They lived in multiple homeless shelters, and even found themselves sleeping in the cold Atlanta streets some days in the winter when the shelters were full.

Eventually, she was able to get on welfare and get a small apartment where she raised my father right in the middle of East Atlanta in the middle of the hood. He survived through the clutches of the ghetto, unscathed, and went on to be one of the greatest attorneys the city had ever seen. Currently, he's running for mayor in Atlanta and everyone knows that he's going to win. The city of Atlanta loves him. And I'm his oldest daughter who has only tried to mimic his steps every day of my life. Which is why it was strange that I hated when people automatically mentioned his name as soon as I said mine. It put on pressure that I wasn't ready for. I didn't want to be measured against his achievements. I just wanted to be me..

"Janelle Pickney…" Chris said again as a smile slowly crept up on his face. "You're George Pickney's—"

"Daughter," I finished for him, pressing my lips in a thin line. "Yes, you're right. I'm his daughter."

Looking away, I began to drum my fingers on the top of the table in front of us while trying my hardest to ignore the fact that all of the other young assistant district attorneys at the table were looking right into my face. I'm sure with expressions of awe or surprise. Either way, I hated it. Plenty of times I'd considered changing my last name just because of the way that they were probably looking at me right now, but I knew it would crush my father once I explained to him why. He'd worked hard for his name… how could I tell him that I didn't want it?

"You probably hate when people mention that, huh?" Chris asked, and I cut my eyes at him, noting the smirk on his face. My stomach did another flip-flop and I thanked God for blessing me with my beautiful dark skin when I felt my cheeks get hot as I nodded my head.

"I understand. My mother is Dr. Harvaty. The big city of Atlanta probably doesn't know of her, but the entire state of Nebraska does. She's an award winning fetal surgeon and I hate constantly being compared to her. How can I ever top a woman who saves babies before they are even born? It's just cruel," he finished with a gentle laugh, laced with a smidgen of exactly the emotion I felt when my achievements were matched against my father's. Finally, somebody understood me. Suddenly, I felt myself begin to smile as a warm feeling settled in my stomach. I liked him.

Before I could say another word, the doors to the left of us, at the head of the courtroom opened up, and in walked a man being held down by two policemen at his arms while another walked ahead of him and another behind. I heard the murmuring in the room as members of the press began to flash their cameras at who I assumed was Luke Murray… AKA Outlaw.

He was tall, had to be easily over six feet, with long curly hair that hung over his face in clumps as they dragged him in. His ankles were cuffed, along with his hands, and even with the oversized orange jumpsuit that he had on, I could tell that he had a muscular build. The crowd began to ripple with conversation as they escorted him in, and suddenly someone said his name. Her voice oozed with lust like a young woman with a high school crush. Luke lifted his head, whipping his mane of hair behind him, and flashed the crowd a smile near the place the voice had come from.

I gasped when I saw that he had a mouth full of sparkly gold teeth.

Then his eyes scanned the crowd and at one point, I felt them land on me. In that infinite moment of time, I felt a stirring heat in my chest as he narrowed his eyes in my face with the corner of his lips pulled up in a sneer. His eyes were wild and vicious. Heated hatred poured through them, like molten lava flowing from a volcano, and traveled directly to my core, stunning me into absolute silence… the kind where even your mind is at a loss for words. I was sitting at the district attorney's table as part of the prosecution. In his mind, I was everything and everyone that was responsible for trying to lock him up for life.

"He looks insane, don't he?" Chris remarked, just as the officers escorted him to his seat across from where we were seated. With my lips pressed firmly together, I nodded and the other assistant district attorneys hummed in agreement.

Dropping my head, I bit my lip pensively as I looked over the details of the case, suddenly even more curious of the malicious and violent acts he had been accused of. From Attorney Pelmington's notes, Luke Murray and his squad of brothers were suspected of committing multiple crimes ranging from grand theft to murder. When I was briefed on the case, I was told that they probably suffered from multiple mental disorders, the primary one being psychopathy from the way that they merciless ran the streets without any real regard for human life.

But I knew better than that. My father had survived the hood and he told my sisters and I about what went on there almost daily. Luke and his brothers were a product of that environment, and I had pledged my life to getting rid of people like him so that others could have a safe place to live.

"All rise for the honorable Judge John Clay Wildon!" the bailiff said, and I eagerly rose to my feet, nearly knocking down my chair in the process.

I felt Chris's hand graze over my back and I looked at him just in time to see him shoot me a comforting smile. Was it that obvious that I was so on edge? And shouldn't he be excited, too? This was our first *real* case!

District Attorney Pelmington stormed over to our table and dropped a clump of papers between the five of us. I looked at him and saw everything I wanted to be in a few years. From my research on him, I learned that it had taken him about five years to get to his status, but I figured that since I'd graduated law school two years early and at the top of my class, if I put in work, I could accomplish what he had in three years instead of five.

"You guys ready?" he whispered to us but it felt more like a statement than a question. What I actually heard was 'you better be ready' because this was it. He turned his back and we pounced on the paperwork on the table, dividing it up between the five of us so that we could be prepared with whatever he may ask for during the trial.

"Okay," the judge began and I snapped my head up to look at him.

I'd already researched him thoroughly and knew everything about his background, including the fact that he happened to be more conservative than liberal... one of the key factors in this case that gave Pelmington an advantage.

"Case number G-10587923, State of New York vs. Luke Murray. Bailiff, have you sworn in the jury?" Judge Wildon asked, peering over his thick glasses. He was pale, bald and old to the point of being ancient. Basically, he looked exactly like any judge you would immediately picture in your mind.

"Yes, your honor," the bailiff answered.

"Okay, then let us begin," Judge Wildon said, looking down at the papers in front of him.

My stomach was bubbling with excitement as I scanned all the faces in front of me. Unable to stop myself, I shot my eyes over to the defense table and looked at Luke Murray from the corner of my eyes.

Does he look like a murderer? I thought as I stared at him, fully taking in his menacing presence.

To be honest, he looked every bit like a few guys I'd seen in Atlanta. Although I went to private school in Alpharetta where a lot of the wealthier people lived, a few times I snuck out with my sister, Carmella, to party on the south side. Those weren't my finest moments. But, hey, I couldn't be the prized child all the time, right?

Somewhere in between me conjuring up the image of Charles Manson and making comparisons between him and Luke Murray, I must have mentally called his name because he turned and looked directly at me. My eyes widened when his stare became a glare, and he pulled back the edge of his lips and snarled at me.

My God, I thought as I pivoted back around and focused on the judge.

He looked crazy. Deranged even. And yes, without a shadow of a doubt, he definitely looked like he could be a murderer.

I kept my attention ahead the entire time after that, not wanting to meet Luke's gaze again for fear that I might turn into dust. Pelmington called his first witness of the day, his primary witness, Jamal Shumpert. He was a weaselly-looking Black man, probably in his mid-twenties, with big eyes like Popeye. He had a few tattoos on his neck, some shapes and symbols that I didn't recognize, and was dressed in skinny jeans and a collared Polo shirt.

Pelmington questioned him like an expert and I felt slightly intimidated, the same way I did when I watched my father's cases. Would I be able to do that? After questioning Jamal, he was able to get him to admit that the victim, Torian Green, had been killed by Luke, and he'd also testified about many other crimes he'd seen him and his brothers commit. Money laundering, drugs, theft… you name it, they did it. They were like the Black Mafia of New York. Jamal was interrogated for nearly an hour, so the judge called a recess to give us all a break before the defense began their cross-examination.

Once court was let out, I ran to the bathroom, peed, grabbed a bottle water, and sat right back down at my seat, eager for everything to begin again. Although the recess was only thirty minutes, it seemed to drag on forever.

"Aye," I heard a voice say from my left, and I felt my whole body begin to prickle, like it does when you're aware someone is speaking to you but silently praying they aren't.

Oh God, I thought, forcing my eyes to remain glued to the paper on the table in front of me. *Please, tell me that's not who I think it is and that he is not talking to me.*

"Aye," he said once more, this time a bit louder than before. "Black-bone, I know ya hear me."

Shit.

Keeping my head down, I glanced over to the left and saw that Luke Murray, the Outlaw himself, was studying me. My attention turned from his face up to the officers standing around him, but they did absolutely nothing. Was he even allowed to talk to me? Wasn't this illegal?

"Aye, after I get out this lil' predicament I'm in… ya think I can take ya to dinner? Naw, you look more like a *brunch* chick. Can I take you to brunch?"

Utterly mortified, I gasped. A few people in the gallery began to laugh around us but Luke simply shrugged and kept his eyes on me. My head snapped back over to one of the officers nearest Luke and, noting the mortified expression on my face, he finally decided to step in.

"Don't talk to the prosecution," he muttered to Luke with an annoyed look like it had taken a great deal of effort to say those words.

"Okay. For real, she not all that anyways. Wit' her black ass," Luke said, and I cut my eyes back at him just in time for him to flash me a smile, showing off all of his gold teeth. Ewe. Just disgusting. His mouth probably tasted like old pennies. The kind you find at the bottom of your sock drawer. He was just all kinds of *yuck*.

After feeling heat on the side of my face for about five full minutes while he stared at me, I decided to get up and wait outside until court was in session again.

"You ready?" Chris said, walking towards me along with another one of the assistant district attorneys. A woman. Cute and blonde with long modelesque legs. Obviously, she was into him from the pained expression on her face that arrived as soon as he stopped to talk to me. No worries, lady, I'm not trying to block you from nabbing one of our most accomplished Black brothas. Do your thing.

"I'm ready," I answered Chris, ignoring the way that the blonde was scrutinizing every part of me. It was obvious that she was trying to figure out if I was a real threat to her. Chris smiled and held out his hand, indicating for me to walk ahead of him and I did just that, taking a deep breath as I walked inside of the courtroom, eager to see the trial continue.

"Defense... are you ready for cross?" Judge Wildon urged once court was in session, and I sat up straight in my seat, more than ready to see what angle the defense was about to take against Pelmington.

"Yes, your honor," Luke's attorney stated, as he stood up and ran his hand over the front of his dress shirt, smoothing out his tie. "The defense is ready to call Jamal Shumpert to the stand for our cross-examination."

It was like you could hear everyone in the courtroom shift in their seats all at the same time, as we all scanned the gallery and waited for the first witness to appear and take the stand again. This was showdown time. The defense was about to try and break apart every bit of Pelmington's case, and I was more than ready for it. Only... where was he?

"Where is he?" Chris muttered my thoughts from next to me, as we both scanned the area behind us.

My lips parted and I sat up a little in my seat, running my eyes over the other bewildered faces behind us as we waited for the first witness of the day to appear. Turning around in my seat, I looked at the other assistant district attorneys, three white girls and a whitish-looking boy, all of their bright eyes muddled with the same curious expression I knew I had in mine as we waited. I licked my lips and turned to Pelmington, instantly calculating the terror building up in his eyes.

"District Attorney Pelmington... where is your witness?" the judge pushed, and I felt my blood go cold when I saw all of Pelmington's drain from his face.

Uht oh. This was *not* good.

"He—he was just here, your honor. I spoke to him right before I walked in. He might be in the restroom. Give me a few minutes so I can give him a call."

And with that, he stormed out, pecking furiously at the screen of his iPhone, his face crimson red. Although I still had a small bit of hope left, it was fleeing by the second.

"This is some shit," Chris spoke from next to me. "Fuckin' witness probably choked up."

He was speaking the words that I was saying in my mind and the same ones that I knew Pelmington had to be thinking along with everyone else in the courtroom. Without Jamal Shumpert being cross-examined, the case would be lost. Judge Wildon would be forced to declare a mistrial, and there would be nothing else Pelmington could do without him since he was the key witness. He was the only one who had actually witnessed what Luke had done on video and with the victim missing, he was the only one who could attest to the fact that he'd been murdered. He was also the only one who could testify about all of the horrid acts committed by the Murray brothers. All was lost.

Biting my lip, I cut my eyes over to the defense table and glanced at Luke once again, totally against my better judgment. But he was much different from before. Obviously, fully convinced that he was about to be let off the hook, he was lying back, nearly in a reclined position in his chair. On his face was a satisfied smirk. Next to him was his attorney, a young, medium-height white guy with short black hair. He was dressed sharply and I could see he was highly paid. Like Luke, he also wore a satisfied smirk on his face. They knew Jamal would not be taking the stand for a second time around.

Seconds later, District Attorney Pelmington stormed in, his face flushed red and his hair tousled all over his head, as if he'd been running his fingers through it repeatedly.

"I—I can't reach him," he admitted with a heavy exhale. "He's not here."

Looking at the downtrodden expression on his face, I couldn't help it. I reacted like a big ass child who had just been told Christmas was cancelled for the year. Tears came to my eyes as I felt my heart drop to the pit of my stomach. The big case that I thought I was going to be seeing had just been washed down the drain.

"Well, without your witness being available for cross, my hands are tied. I have no other choice but to declare this trial a mistrial," the judge explained, and Pelmington dropped his head as he stood in front of him, his shoulders drooped, making him appear shrunken in stature.

"I know. Thank you, your honor."

"Bullshit," Chris said, clicking his teeth. I brushed away a tear that had escaped from my eyes, hoping he didn't see it.

"Well," Judge Wildon began, licking his lips while pushing his glasses up on his nose. "I'm declaring this a mistrial. Court is dismissed. I'm instructing that the defendant be let free and the jury dismissed. Thank you, jury, for your time. I sincerely appreciate—"

"Noooo," I mumbled as I shook my head. "This can't be."

"Unfortunately, it is," Pelmington said as he walked over and began snatching up the papers that he'd dropped on the table. "You all go on home. We're done for now."

He turned to leave as cameras flashed in his face. A storm of journalists and photographers followed on his heels, asking questions that I was sure pissed him off.

"Well, justice has been served," Chris said, sucking his teeth as he stood up. He held his hand out to help me up and I took it.

"Has it?" I asked, glancing over to where Luke Murray was still sitting, chatting with his attorney. Probably congratulating him on a job well done.

"I LOVE YOU, LUKE!" a girl yelled out from the back of the gallery. She was the same one who had called his name earlier.

"I love you, too, baby," Luke shot back at her with a thick southern accent, a wink and a lopsided smile.

I looked over at the girl who was standing at the back of the courtroom dressed like she was headed to the nearest club, in a bandage dress and four-inch heels with long weave cascading down her back. Under my eye, she blew him a kiss and I paddled my eyes to him just in time to see him shoot her one back.

Sick, I thought as I rolled my eyes.

Fresh out of the roll, my pupils settled right on Luke who was watching me with a smirk on his face. Shit. He'd caught the eye roll and now he was laughing at me. Oh God, I didn't know him and couldn't stand him all at the same time.

"Let's go," Chris said, reminding me that he was still standing there. "You wanna get a drink?"

"Sure," I agreed, turning my back to Luke even though his face was still etched in my mind.

"Can I come too?" Blondy asked from the other side of Chris, her flirty tone sickening to my ears.

I fought the urge to roll my eyes again, as I watched the way that she ducked her head and smiled all bashfully when Chris nodded, agreeing to allow her to tag along. Then he turned around to walk to the door, with Blondy hot on his heels, talking excitedly about something that was probably just as stupid as she looked.

And that's how I became the third wheel. This was beginning to be the most fucked up of all fucked up days.

About Me.

Janelle

*A*t twenty-three years old, I was about two years younger than all of the other students in my class when I graduated. Being my father's oldest of four daughters, I always felt the desire to be most like him. I admired him. Like every little girl given the pleasure of growing up with her father, he was my hero. My mother died from ovarian cancer when I was in high school, leaving my father to raise me and my three other sisters. There were a lot of us but we were all close being that, after me, each of my sisters had been born in two-year intervals. Each one even prettier than the next.

Carmella was just underneath me, only two years younger. She was curvy and thick in all the right places, with medium-brown skin and an ass that many chicks in Atlanta paid for. But hers was 'all naturalllllle' as she reminded everyone on the daily. She was in school to be a chemist but spent most of her time being an Instagram model. She was twenty-one and should have been about to graduate with her Bachelors, but she only had enough credits to be considered a sophomore because she was more interested in flashing pics and being paid to model boutique clothes than anything else.

Then there was Mixie. Her real name was Maxine but she hated the name and, from the time she could talk, always referred to herself as Mixie so the name stuck. She got her looks from our mother who was part Black (Jamaican), part Hispanic (Puerto Rican) and part white (Italian). Mixie had a fair-skin tone with greenish eyes that dazzled anyone who looked into them. Although she was always complimented for her looks, she didn't rely on them to get her ahead. At nineteen, she had her heart set on being a doctor and was the sister most like me. She worked hard but she also played hard. She was outgoing and played sports, rendering her an athletic scholarship as well as an academic scholarship once it was time for her to go to college.

Last was Vonia, full-name TreVonia. She was the youngest at seventeen and was in her senior year of high school. She was a perfect mixture of both my mother and my father, being blessed with a beautiful dark mahogany complexion and my mother's hazel eyes that gave her an exotic allure. Donned the 'turn up Queen', there wasn't a party happening in Atlanta that she wasn't attending. She was a handful and got away with things that I'd never even *thought* about doing but, being my parents' youngest, they were just about done by the time they got to her and were simply happy that she always made it home alive.

Then there was me. I was the oldest of the clan. I got my looks and brains from my father. I was what they called a 'dark-skinned beauty' but I hated being referred to as that. Why couldn't I just be beautiful? It was just like this current society to assume that having dark skin and being beautiful was an anomaly. Like the two couldn't *possibly* exist together. I hated that shit. I wasn't 'pretty for a dark-skinned chick', I was just pretty. Damn it!

Anyways, I had my father's dark, mocha-colored skin, with short natural hair that maintained its length right at my shoulders, no matter how many Hair Infinity vitamins I took. I wasn't curvy and thick like Carmella, didn't have green eyes like Mixie or hazel ones like Vonia. I was slim build with about a handful of tits and just nearly a bit more ass and dark brown eyes. I did have longer lashes than any of my sisters so that's one thing I had over them all! I was also the smartest and I waved that fact around like a flag.

"So, is this how you always end a long day of work?" Blondy asked Chris using the same annoying, flirty tone that I'd started to think was just her normal voice.

We were at a bar across the street from the courthouse having drinks. It wasn't a bad spot and I could definitely see myself coming here pretty often after a long day in court. The atmosphere was nice, it was piled high with a lot of professionals who probably worked in the area, and the music was pleasant. The drinks sucked, but I guess you couldn't have it all.

Sipping on my margarita, I watched as Blondy leaned into Chris, placing her chin on her fist as if she was waiting on him to give her life. I was utterly disgusted at how thirsty she was. Obviously, she was brilliant. Wasn't bad in the looks department. Okay… I guess I'm hating a bit. She was beautiful. She had the looks department on lock with her blonde hair, tanned skin, and sparkling baby blues. But she was past thirsty. She was *parched*. She was throwing herself at him to the point that she might as well have been wearing a 'fuck me now' sign.

"Not usually. But if I have to sit through too many more cases like that, I'll start," he replied with a shrug.

As if he'd told the world's funniest joke, Blondy started to laugh.

The sound of her laughter annoyed me even more than her voice. I couldn't take this any longer. Draining my glass, I pulled out a few bills from my pocket and tossed them on the counter next to my drink and started to gather my things.

"Thanks for inviting me out for drinks," I said to Chris, as I placed my laptop bag on my shoulder. "I have to get back home so I can brush up on a few things… you know, so I can be prepared for the rest of the week."

I was shocked when I saw Chris's face flash with disappointment. Why he seemed so sad about me leaving, I had no idea. Since we'd gotten there, him and Blondy had been totally engrossed in conversation and I hadn't said more than two words beyond answering a few questions he'd asked me… probably because he felt sorry for having me sit there practically alone. Either way, I was about to do both of them a favor and get lost.

"You're leaving already?" Chris asked, and I nodded my head, cutting my eyes at his fan who was smiling up at me. She was ecstatic to see me go.

"Yeah, I have some things I need to catch up on," I repeated, rubbing a stray strand of hair from my face.

"Aw, that's too bad," Blondy added, pulling out her best impression of a sad face. Thank God she'd taken on law and not acting because she was terrible at it.

"Well, let me walk you out."

"It's okay, I'm only—"

Before I could finish my sentence, Chris had grabbed my hand

and tugged me by his side. I felt butterflies fluttering around in the pit of my stomach, as I clamped my mouth closed and allowed him to guide me to the door. The palm of my hands began to get clammy as my nervousness built up inside of me, making my entire body warm.

Shit. C'mon, Janelle. Sweating is not cute.

We walked outside of the double doors and then Chris stopped, turning so that he was standing right in front of me. He was still holding my hand and all of my senses were so concentrated on that fact that I couldn't even birth a single thought in my mind. Finally, he let go and I mentally exhaled, as my brain functions slowly begin to work once again.

"Can I get your number?" he asked, then licked his lips. My knees got weak as I silently thanked God for the cool air making his lips dry. Shit… were my lips dry too? I wet my dry lips and nearly fainted when I saw Chris's eyes go to my tongue.

"Um… yes," I answered him. "You want me to write it down?"

"Naw, you can put it in my phone," he said, as he handed me the iPhone in his pocket. I grabbed it and stopped to look at the screen for a second. It was a picture of him and a little boy who looked just like him. He was probably about two years old. His son?

"You have a son?" I asked before I could stop the words from coming out of my mouth.

"No," he laughed and my chest got tight. "My nephew."

"Oh," I said, and then pecked my phone number into his phone, saving it under my name. I handed the phone back to him and his hand brushed mine when he grabbed it. My face got so warm it almost burned. He looked at the screen of his phone and started pressing on buttons while I took the opportunity to continue staring at him. Then my phone began to vibrate in my pocket.

"Oh, I need to get this," I told him as I reached down to grab my phone. "It's probably my dad calling to see if—"

I paused and frowned at the screen when I saw that it was a number I didn't recognize.

"Nope. It's just me," Chris told me with a light chuckle. "Now you have my number."

"Oh," I mumbled. Duh… Now I just felt stupid.

"Here's a cab," Chris said as he raised his hand and flagged it down. The cab screeched to a stop and pulled over right in front of us. I guess it wasn't all that hard for a Black man in New York City to hail a cab. Well, not one as sexy as Chris anyways.

"Hope to see you around more often," he told me as he walked over and opened the cab door.

"Uh, m—me too," I stammered as I started to get in. "I mean… I hope to see you around more… never mind."

Smiling, Chris closed the door of the cab and I turned quickly away, hoping that he couldn't see the embarrassment on my face. It wasn't until the driver began to roll away that I finally let out the breath I'd been holding.

What a day.

Tits n Ass Show.

Outlaw

"*I* wanna see muthafuckin' bottles poppin' up in this bitch! I'm home, muthafuckas!" I yelled as I stomped inside of the club for the welcome home party that my brothers had thrown for me.

I was fresh out after being held up in county for over three months over some bullshit. One of my homegirls had gotten raped by some fuck nigga by the name of Torian Green. After she told me, I handled that shit A-muthafuckin'-SAP. Gave that nigga a permanent dirt nap, if you catch my drift. The fucked up part about it as that I'd been caught on security camera, but I wasn't too worried about that shit because they ain't catch me doing nothing but whooping Torian's ass.

But then a few weeks later after he'd gone 'missing', they'd cased my homeboy Jamal up on some petty shit and threatened to toss him back in the pen for violating probation. So, what did that nigga do? His ass turned snitch and I got stuck with a case.

But now, after making sure word got to Jamal that my niggas had found out where his mama and aunty was hiding at, I was free once again. Life was sweet. But pussy was sweeter and that's exactly what I was in the mood for as I scanned the club.

"Heeyyyyy, Outlaw," a chick sang as she walked in front of me, just slow enough for me to get a good look at her tight body and fat ass.

Shawty was thick and had big ass dick-sucking lips. Just what I needed for the night. But I wasn't stingy with my meat, na' mean? I liked to share the love so her ass had to get on the list with about five other shawties that I would be taking back to the crib.

"Wassup, lil' mama?" I asked, flashing her my golds while grabbing my dick. She knew what time it was but, just in case, I was letting her know.

"Oooh shit, I just love that southern accent," her homegirl enthused from behind her, and I shot her a look, taking in her full appearance in just under three seconds. She was bowlegged with big ole titties. Yep, she could get it too.

"Can I keep you company tonight?" the first girl asked. "Help welcome you home?"

"Hell yeah, shawty," I told her as I licked my lips. "Bring ya homegirl, too." I nudged my chin at the girl standing with her, and she smiled deeply then stood up straight, making sure to poke out her ass. Not necessary. I'd already peeped it all.

"I'll get at y'all later. Meet me at the whip when this shit over if you ain't on no bullshit," I instructed them before winking one eye and walking away. It was time for me to go chill, turn up, and blow trees with my niggas. My muthafuckin' brothers.

"Wassup, bro?!" my oldest brother, Kane, said as he stood up and dapped me up.

"Naw, nigga, hit me up wit' a hug," I told him, laughing as I reached out and hugged him tight, patting him square on the back. "My ass was almost cased up for life, son. Glad y'all niggas came through in the clutch."

"Don't we always?" Tank said, his deep voice barely audible over the thumping speakers in the club. "You know we wasn't gon' just be chillin' and shit with our lil' nigga lookin' at life in chain gang, nigga. We got'cho back."

"I know it," I told him, nodding my head as I reached over to give him a hug.

Tank was the next oldest under Kane, who was like a father figure to us all. Not like we didn't have a father because we did. Yeah, most people saw us and thought that we were six niggas who were blood through our mother only and all had different daddies, but nope. My brothers and I were the product of two people who loved each other. Two people who loved each other and tried desperately to give birth to a girl before giving up on that dream once they ended up with my ass.

"Where Yolo?" I asked, referring to another brother. Looking over, I noticed that Tank and Kane had both already started to light up. I breathed in deeply, inhaling the pungent odor of the good ass weed I was used to. In county, I smoked one every day, but they didn't have the good shit in there that I could get my hands on out here.

"Doc probably out lining up some bitches to parade in front of your ass. You know he gotta make sure you stocked up for the night," Tank said, shaking his head. "That nigga on one for real, yo. He actually gave the bouncers a fuckin' checklist to go through before they decide to let a bitch in. Calls it the 'no basic bitch' list. That nigga stupid!"

Laughing, I sat down next to Tank and grabbed the blunt from his fingers just at the exact time that my favorite brother walked up. Well, I couldn't say that he was my favorite because I loved all my niggas. But *this* nigga right here was my dude. Cree aka Dent, but to me, he would always be known as FatBoy because he was chubby as hell when we were younger. It wasn't until he hit puberty and his nuts dropped that he began to shed the weight. Now he was tall and muscular, similar to me, but I didn't give a fuck. In my mind, he would always be Fat.

"Yo, Fat! What's *up*, my nigga?!" I yelled shooting up from where I was sitting to grab him up in a hug.

"Yoooo, my nigga home. Shiiiit… everybody in this bitch better turn da fuck uuuup," Cree said and I frowned as I looked at him.

"Nigga, you leanin'?" I asked him with a smile. "You operatin' in slow mo."

"Yeah, I'm on that good shit, nigga. This new recipe that Doc whipped up. I brought you some," he told me, pulling a miniature ketchup bottle out of his pocket. I grabbed it and brought it up eye-level.

"This lil' bitty shit got you actin' like that?" I asked him, chuckling to myself as I eyed the pink liquid.

"Nigga, dat's all you *neeeeed*," Cree replied back and I cracked the hell up looking at his ass. His eyes were barely open. Like there was no way he could even see me. My nigga was *fucked up* for real, but he was on a glorious high. The 'nobody can ever fuck up my day' kinda high. I squinted at the bottle one more time and shook the liquid inside. This had to be some good shit. Coming from Doc, I knew it had to be.

And this, for the most part, was my fam. My primary niggas who I would give my life for. The only muthafuckas on the planet who I knew wouldn't hesitate to give theirs for me. Kane, Tank, Cree and Yolo. We also had another brother who was in between Tank and Cree. His name was Tone but he'd been killed some years back when I was still a jit. Kane and Tank took care of that shit though. The niggas who killed him were only a bad memory by the time they were done.

Kane, the oldest, took that role very seriously. The nigga stayed ridin' my ass about some shit. Kane was the reason why every single one of us were college educated. My brothers and I busted the thug stereotype wide open because all of us had a degree with our name on it. Kane set the example. When I was still in middle school, charming the panties off every girl who would pay me any attention, he was taking classes at the University of Georgia, getting a degree in Business Administration with a specialization in Finance. After he graduated, he also studied real estate and he was the reason why we all had properties around the country in our names.

After Kane graduated, he made it known that he would fuck us up if we didn't follow in his footsteps, so we did. Tank got a degree in criminology. Cree became a dentist, which is the reason for his nickname 'Dent' and Yolo, which was actually short for 'Young Yellow', something our Big Mama called him because of his fair skin, got his degree in pharmacology. We used to call him 'Doc' when he was younger because he was always trying to whip up some magic potion for us to drink whenever we were sick. He got that shit from my grandmother, who was always pulling some roots and herbs out her backyard, calling herself curing a nigga. Yolo was currently trying to figure out if he wanted to pursue a medical degree and I was all for that shit. He'd been acting like a doctor for as long as I knew him… might as well make it official, right?

And then there was me. Luke 'Outlaw' Murray, the youngest of the Murray brothers. I had attended and graduated from University of Miami with an engineering degree, before getting an online master's degree from New York University in Information Technology, which was a fancy way of saying I could hack into *a lot* of shit.

You probably thought we were a bunch of stupid ass thugs with a coke-addicted mother who used to sell pussy for rocks, before coming home and fuckin' some random nigga in her roach infested apartment in the middle of the Pork 'n' Bean projects while we ran the streets wild, robbing convenience stores and hunching girls under a bridge, huh? Nope... that's not us. Well, I've done some thangs with a chick or two under a bridge, but I ain't never *hunch* nothing. If the clothes came off, somebody was about to get this dick, pronto.

We came from a middle-class family in Miami, but every summer we were shipped across the country to New York to spend it with our grandmother, Big Mama, who lived in the Brooklyn projects. We lived for the summer. As soon as the soles of our feet touched down in New York city, we became straight thugs, snatchin' panties and whoopin' asses wherever we went. We ran the streets like devils, making trouble wherever we went.

By the time I hit high school, Cree was a Junior and the others had graduated, so Cree and I convinced our folks to let us stay with our grandmother so we could help take care of her, and that was the end of that prep school shit. What was natural to us finally came out into the open, and the thug in all of us began to permanently shine through.

My pops was always talking about how much of a disappointment we were to him, using our education in order to take control of the streets, but I wasn't concerned with what he had to say. His ass was whack anyways. He had been born in the hood and left it to get on that Cliff Huxtable shit. That wasn't me.

"There go my nigga." I grinned from ear-to-ear when I saw Yolo walking in with a band of bad bitches parading behind him.

Bruh had put in work for sure. Every time I looked at one, I knew she would be one of the ones I'd be taking home, until I looked at the next one in line. They were all sexy as hell and I couldn't choose. But why should I? Was it a crime to take them all? And did I really care if it was? Hell naw!

"Damn, Outlaw, hurry up and pick your poison, nigga, 'cuz I got next!" Cree said, as he stood up to get a better look at the chicks as Yolo led them over to where we sat in a makeshift V.I.P. area.

"I'mma make this easy on all y'all. I'll take the first five," I decided as I ran my eyes over them.

It was like getting a little bit of everything. The first one was a banging ass Black chick with a big ghetto booty. The second looked like she could be Spanish or some shit, but her body was on point, too. The third was a red bone with thick legs and a big ass; the one behind her was exactly the same, but brown-skinned, and the last one was a fly ass Asian chick.

"A'ight, my baby brother just got outta county and I wanna make sure that he's shown a good time. Who up for dat shit?" Yolo asked, and all the chicks put their hands in the air while making their best fuck faces at me.

"Well, he gon' need some help deciding who he goin' home with, so I need y'all to help him out. The DJ gon' play a song and I need y'all to twerk that shit out to the end. Show him what he'll be gettin' if it's up to you," Yolo instructed, and they all began to nod their heads, smiling and hi-fiving each other as they prepared to get their moves in order. The DJ started to drop the beat on a dance track, and they went to work. It was ass and titties flying everywhere. A tits 'n ass show.

"Damn, nigga," I told Yolo, dapping him up as he walked over to where I was and sat down. "You really came through for a nigga."

"Aye, that's the least I can do. Welcome home, fam," he said, giving me a half-hug before sitting down next to Cree who looked like he was damn near sleep. I punched him in the shoulder to see if he was awake.

"Yoooo, niggaaa," he said slowly, rubbing his upper arm. "I'm tryna enjoy the shooowww!"

"That nigga on that good shit. Doc, what you give him?" Kane asked, looking at Yolo.

"I liquidized some weed, stirred it in the lean, and dropped some other shit in it to make it taste good," he replied with a shrug and ran his hand over his low-cut fade. "Ain't shit."

"Well, I got me some so I'll let you know how that shit is after I get me some," I told him, waving the bottle that Cree had given to me. Yolo grinned and then nodded his head.

"Yeah, let me know what you think, bruh."

I turned back around just in time to see the thick brown-skinned chick drop it low into a spit before bouncing up and down while grinding her booty, straight showing me how she would ride the dick. My man went rock hard in my pants and I was ready to go. Opening up the small bottle, I tossed my head back and drained it completely.

"A'ight, fam. I'm out this bitch," I told Yolo as I stood up and said goodbye to each of my brothers. After that, I pointed at the five girls I wanted to take with me and they squealed in excitement as they followed me out to my whip. Then I got another surprise when I saw the two shawties I'd hit up coming in, standing there waiting for me.

"Damn… it's gon' be a hell of a night," I said to myself.

I jumped in the driver's side and they squeezed in the back of my red Camaro. I had a strict 'no bitch in the front seat' rule, and I was serious about that shit. I had no chicks in my front seat unless it was my mama or Big Mama. You wanna know why? It was simple.

I was superstitious.

Yeah, it sounds crazy and if a muthafucka ever said it, I'd die denying that shit, but it was true. I was superstitious to a fault. And the reality was, every nigga in my family ended up getting the first chick to ride in their front seat pregnant. Every. Single. One.

My pops had taken my moms out for their first date in the first car he ever owned and six months later, she was pregnant with Kane. Kane had a baby by a chick he was messing with in college. He bought his first car, let her ride shotgun, and she turned up pregnant. Same thing happened with Tank and Yolo, but Yolo's chick lost her baby before giving birth. Cree didn't have a car because he didn't think it made sense since he lived in the city, and I'd just purchased my whip about a year before getting locked up when I decided to grab a spot back in Brooklyn to be closer to Big Mama. Since then, no woman has ridden in the passenger side of my shit.

"Outlaw, are all the rumors about you true?" one of the girls asked, and I glanced at her through the rearview mirror, smiling when she blew me a kiss and licked her lips. I laughed but didn't answer.

"Yeah, I heard that you break bitches' backs and shit wit' that monster you holdin' in your pants…" another one teased, flashing me her pearly white teeth.

Not backs, but I have broken a bed or two, I thought but didn't say a word. I didn't brag on my dick like other niggas because I didn't feel the need to. They would find out what a nigga was working with soon enough.

Freak-a-Leek.

Janelle

"*J*anelllleeeee, you know I love you, right?" my roommate, Val, said right after I stumbled into our apartment.

That one margarita I drank had a late effect. I thought it was weak but it was just the opposite. If I had stayed at the bar long enough to order another one, I would have been rolling out on my ass.

"Whatever it is, the answer is no," I told Val, dropping my bags on the couch before ambling over to the kitchen to grab some water to flush the alcohol out my system. I definitely needed to get my head right before Val started with her bullshit of the day.

Valerie was something like a friend but not quite because we were just so different. I tolerated her... yeah, that's more like it. She and I started out at NYU at the same damn time, but she was still struggling to finish her bachelor's degree. She'd changed her major five times before deciding that she wanted to be a psychologist. But with some of the stuff she did, I felt like *she* was the one who needed to get *her* head checked instead of the other way around. Val was always sleeping around. It was like she never had a nigga smiling in her face who she didn't eventually have sex with.

I definitely wasn't a virgin and I wasn't ashamed about that fact either. I loved dick, I loved men, and I loved sex, but I had some discretion about who I slept with. Val? Not at all. If he paid her the least bit of attention, he had earned his way into her panties. And, eleven times out of ten, I was the one left helping her out of those situations, whether it was a trip to the clinic for some pills or an abortion. She just never learned.

"Janelle, *please,* I really need your help on this one. Remember Rodney?"

She stormed in on me just as I was walking out of the kitchen, placing every bit of her 5'4, slim-thick, wide-hipped and flat-tummied frame in my face. I glanced at the eager, pleading expression on her face and couldn't resist her gentle Bambi eyes. Val was gorgeous, but she had terrible self-esteem… or maybe it was just daddy issues. Her father had left her and her mother to pursue his budding football career when she was only three years old.

Although she spoke of it like she was unaffected, the fact that she was constantly jumping into bed with any man who paid her any attention told me otherwise. I couldn't wait until they covered daddy issues and relationships in one of her psychology classes, so I could pop a mirror right in front of her face and show her exhibit A for her first case study on what it meant to live your life searching for some man to play the role of daddy.

"Yes, I remember Rodney, Val," I muttered, pushing by her as I twisted the cap off of my water bottle. She was hot on my heels, stomping heavily even though she probably only weighed about 125 pounds soaking wet.

"Well… I thought that we were a thing but I guess he didn't," she started. I sat down on the couch and pulled my legs up under my body, getting comfortable so I could hear the rest of her story.

"What makes you think he didn't?" I asked, although I already could guess the reason. Rodney never did anything but chill on our couch with her and watch about fifteen minutes of movies before pushing up on her and whining about going to the room so they could have sex. He was never anything other than a slobbery, greasy and, most importantly, *broke* bootycall.

Val let out a heavy sigh and flopped down on the chair in front of me, raising her knees up so that her chin could rest on top of them.

"Because he burned me. He was sleeping with someone else and now... I think I got an STD."

"WHAT?!" I shrieked, dropping my water bottle in the process. Water spilled everywhere so I stooped over to grab the bottle back up, stamping the leftover water into the carpet with my foot.

"What do you mean he *burned* you? You had sex with him without a condom? How could you be so stupid, Val—I've told you about this before! What were you thinking?" I asked her, my tone more accusing than anything else.

Val shot me a sheepish look before dropping her eyes and slumping over, cradling her legs with her arms. A single tear fell down her cheek and I instantly felt guilty for being so hard on her. And just like that, she had me. Whatever she needed me to do was going to get done.

"Like I said... I thought we were a thing," she replied quietly.

"What do you need?" I asked her. My thoughts ran rapid in my mind. I wanted to ask her if she'd gotten officially tested… how did she know what kind of STD she had? It could be AIDS! Oh God… what if she had AIDS?!

"It's gonorrhea. I know because I've had it before." She flinched with her admission, visually making me aware of her shame. "I entered a prescription for it into the system at my job, but I put it under your name so that it couldn't get traced back to me. If they found out I filled a fake prescription, I'd get fired so I just need you to pick it up."

Frowning, I felt a flare of heat rise in my chest as I thought about what she was saying. A trip to the clinic was one thing but this shit… this was too much. How could she put a prescription for gonorrhea in *my* name? I'd never had an STD in my life and the last thing I wanted was to have anyone think that. What if I was trying to be a judge one day and someone happened to stumble on these medical records, drudging up a past of whoredom that I'd never quite had—their only proof being that I'd had been prescribed medication to treat gonorrhea? Yes, I know. I went way out there and the possibility of that ever happening was probably little to none, but still!

"Val, why didn't you just go to the clinic like you usually—" I stopped, biting down hard on my bottom lip right as I thought out how harsh the rest of my sentence would have sound.

"Like I usually do?" Val finished for me, narrowing her eyes. Then her glare softened and she ducked her head down. It sounded bad but it was the truth. She'd been in this situation a few times and a trip to the clinic had always been her cure.

"I didn't want to go anymore… the last time I went in there, the lady at the front desk knew me by name. I can't go in there anymore," she finished quietly. "I work at the pharmacy so I thought it would be easier to just do it this way."

Pressing my lips together, I choked down my natural urge to want to reprimand her about her decisions and chastise her for once again putting herself at risk, and pushed myself to just be a great friend.

"I'll do it."

Standing up, I walked over and placed my hand on her shoulder, rubbing it gently and hoping that this would be my final time going to the pharmacy to grab medication for an STD.

***

"I'm here to pick up a prescription for Janelle Pickney, please," I mumbled, barely above a whisper, as I stood at the counter of the pharmacy that Val worked at.

It was only about two blocks away from where we stayed, but every bit of the way walking there, I was reminded of the fact that we lived right in the hood. Although my father had more than enough money to make sure that I was staying in a high-rise apartment in Manhattan, I refused his help. I was used to getting things on my own because I felt better about being able to say that I'd worked hard and bought my own shit. Not to mention, I'd gone all through law school being made to feel like I was only there because of who he was and not because of my own abilities. I didn't need any more handouts from daddy.

So after searching around for a place that we could afford, Val and I settled on a nice, comfortable, quaint—in New York talk, 'quaint' means small as hell—apartment in Brooklyn. The commute to school had taken me hours each day, and the commute to work was no better, but it was a place we could afford and the block that we were on was nice and no one bothered us. There was very little crime and I enjoyed the fact that we lived around a mixture of different cultures.

But this pharmacy? It was something straight out of a movie. Homeless people set up residence right outside on the sidewalks leading up to it, junkies leaned and danced on each corner, boosters walked around selling all kinds of stolen shit from behind their leather jackets and… I was even certain that I'd seen a pimp slap a bitch. Okay, that last one was an exaggeration but I didn't doubt that it could happen.

"Here you go," the older man at the counter said as he handed me over a white bag that a younger Black man behind the counter had given to him.

Squinting through his Coke-bottle glasses, he leaned over and peered at the label on the bag making my cheeks heat up with embarrassment. I glanced behind me, hoping there was no one standing around watching. Thankfully, besides a couple sitting down at a booth checking their blood pressure, we were alone.

"Let's make sure we have the right prescription. These are two medications. One for Ceftriaxone and the other for Azithromycin. Both are used to treat the same thing. Do you know for what?"

My mouth went completely dry to the point that I couldn't move my tongue. So instead, I just dropped my chin a bit and let my mouth gape open. I probably resembled a fish. I glanced at the guy behind him who shot a look in my direction with his brows raised before going back to what he was doing.

"Um… yes, I—how much do I owe for it?" I finally was able to sputter out.

"Oh, you don't owe a thing. This type of stuff is free… lucky for you, huh?" the old guy asked, leaning over as he wiggled his eyebrows at me. I've never been so embarrassed in my life.

Reaching out, I grabbed the bag from his hands and whirled around to leave, just as the door at the front opened, signaling the bell alarm to chime. I looked up and nearly peed in my pants when I saw who it was, trampling inside of the pharmacy, his head bent down as he looked at something on his phone. It was Luke Murray. The Outlaw… the one I'd seen in court only the day before. But what was he doing here?

He looked different but I recognized him instantly. He was dressed in much nicer clothes than the orange jumpsuit I'd seen him in before. His long, curly mane was braided down in a fly style, with the long ends of his hair falling down behind him. He'd gotten a nice lil' edge, taming his facial hair that was ragged and overgrown in court but, even with his head down, I knew it was him. It was almost like I could feel him and it immediately ignited a strong, stirring emotion inside of me. Something in between dangerous curiosity and fear.

He moved like he was about to raise his head and I immediately ducked off to the side into the next aisle over, pretending like I was looking for something.

Shit, I cursed when I realized that I was on the family planning aisle. I was holding a prescription for gonorrhea and now I was eye level with a display of condoms. How tactful of me.

"Aye, nigga, wassup?!" Luke greeted someone, I assumed the younger man who had been behind the counter.

"Outlaw! What you doin' here, young'in?" the pharmacist replied to my utter astonishment. He knew Luke Murray? Damn!

"I'm fresh out and came to pick up my regular… you got that?"

Hmm… his regular. Pursing my lips, I stared at a box of Trojan Magnums in front of me as I wondered what his regular was.

"I sure do! Here you go. Had it waitin' on ya," the old man replied, just as I remembered I needed to be getting the hell out of there.

Biting my bottom lip, I side-stepped a few paces down until I felt I was at a safe enough distance to stand up and hightail it out of there. I neared the corner of the aisle, finally deciding to stand up and bolt to the door, when I ran right smack into a brick wall, knocking the medication and my purse right out of my hand.

"Oh, sorry!" I yelled out when I realized the wall had feet and was actually a person.

It wasn't until I had snatched up my purse from the floor that I realized the feet in front of me were donning red and white sneakers adorned with stars and rhinestone diamonds… and they belonged to Luke Murray.

Shit. Shit. Shit!

"Damn, shawty, where you in a hurry to?" he asked me, catching my eyes right as I looked away. I saw his fill with recognition right before I was able to duck my head. But it was too late. He knew exactly who I was. Biting my lip, I exhaled heavily before raising my head and looking him square in the face.

"Aye, I know you..." he continued, his eyes twinkling with... humor? "Black-bone."

Without answering him, I scanned the floor for the prescription for a few seconds before painstakingly realizing it was right in his hands.

"This yours?" he asked, reading the label. "Shit... you lawyer chicks be getting down, huh?"

I felt like I wanted to open up a crack in the ground and slip myself right through it.

"That's not mine," I told him, attempting to snatch the bag from his hands. He moved it out of my grasp, clicking his teeth in a taunting, but playful way. What a jerk.

"I got it for a friend."

His expression shifted and I felt like he was smiling although he wasn't. It was all in his eyes and that damn way his upper lip curled upwards showing off his disgusting gold teeth. He was laughing at me on the inside. I could feel it.

"A friend, huh?" he asked, and then his eyes darted to my nametag hanging from the waist of my dark grey pencil skirt. You know... the one I used to get access into the building at work. The one that said Janelle Pickney in bold, black, big ass letters.

"A friend with the same name?" he quipped, the edge of his upper lip turning up once more until it eased its way into a full-on smirk.

"Why don't you just mind your business?" I mumbled, snatching the bag from his hand as I began to storm out of the pharmacy. I didn't stop until I got outside and realized that my path across the street was blocked by the presence of a fiery red Camaro, illegally parked in the front of the store. One guess who it belonged to.

"You know, I could've asked you to mind your own business yesterday when you was tryin' to get a nigga cased up. But did I do that? Noooo. I asked ya stuck up ass out for brunch," he shot out from behind me, making me roll my eyes.

"You mean right before you said I wasn't all that with my Black ass?" I tilted my head and placed my hands on my hips. He laughed and I couldn't help but notice he had a nice smile.

"Yeah, but I prefer dark-skinned chi—"

"And what do you mean, 'mind *my* business'? You were on trial for committing a slew of violent crimes!" I countered.

The lawyer in me gave me a natural urge to argue any point that I was trying to make, something I'd done since I was a child without any regard as to who I was arguing it to. And I was going to continue on with my present conversation when I was suddenly reminded of what some of the crimes Luke was accused of were. The boldest one standing out in my mind: Murder.

Shut up, Janelle, I thought, squashing my urge to debate. *Shut up and leave. This dude is crazy.*

"I ain't do none of that shit they said I did!" he replied, emphatically. I cut my eyes to him and saw that he was wearing the same expression he had in the pharmacy. Laughing eyes with his upper lip curled up.

He was lying his ass off.

"For real, yo! I'm a good honest citizen!"

For some reason, I decided to humor him. Maybe it was because one glance at my watch told me I'd already missed my train and would have to wait another fifteen minutes before I could catch another.

"A good honest citizen," I repeated, then pointed my eyes at his car. "With no job on record. How can you afford a ride like this?"

There was a brief pause and then he smirked, walked over to the side of the car and crossed his arms as he stood in front of it.

"If I tell you da truth 'bout me… you ain't gon' believe dat shit," he began and licked his lips. Gold teeth flashed before my eyes. Yuck.

"Humor me," I battled, crossing my arms in front of my own chest as I peered at him.

"Well," he started, his southern drawl growing even stronger by the second. "I got a degree in Engineering from the University of Miami and a master's in IT from NYU."

Silence hung between us as I glared at him, wondering how stupid he thought I was, while I waited for him to tell me the truth. But he only gazed at me with a lop-sided smile on his face. The one that he must've thought was sexy but had no effect whatsoever on me. Not any worth mentioning anyways.

"Whatever. I gotta go," I shot back, rolling my eyes as I took off, checking both ways before I left him and trotted across the street.

"Aye, can I get ya number? I might need some legal advice!" he called out but I ignored him. Even still, his words made me smile. Legal advice? Yeah right. He seemed to have that area on lock after beating us in court yesterday.

Either way, I'd already spent way too much time talking to someone that could have cost me my job if my boss ever found out. The last thing I was ever going to do was give him my number. Even if I was attracted to him, which I was absolutely, *positively* not. He was gross. Covered with tattoos and dressed like a rap star, when the men I preferred donned tailor-made suits. Not to mention those hideous gold teeth. Ewe.

No, he was definitely not my type at all.

Pretty Boy.

Janelle

Much to my excitement, I was able to spend another day with Chris. Much to my disappointment, Blondy was there, too.

"Yesterday was a letdown," Pelmington began, and I clasped my hands together in front of my face, watching him intensely, hanging onto his every word. "It was the first of many letdowns that you'll face as an attorney. Learn from it."

He paused and I felt the hair on my neck rise up, and I shifted in my seat just as I was hit with the sudden notion that someone was watching me. I turned to my right and caught myself staring right into Chris's eyes. He smiled and it lit a fire in the pit of my stomach. Bashfully, I shot him a smile back before going back to Pelmington.

"Today, I brought something for you," he turned, swiping his arm over a table covered with a seemingly endless supply of folders. "These are all the cases I've lost in all the time I've been practicing law. I want you all to divide these up and take them home. Study them and then be prepared to come back sometime soon and tell me how you would have won the case."

Before he could even finish his instructions, I had to bite down on my bottom lip to stop myself from squealing with excitement. Yes, I was a nerd, a huge one, but I made a choice a while ago to simply embrace the fact.

As soon as Pelmington walked out of the room, closing the door behind him, I jumped right up and dashed over to the table, eager to have first pick of the files. I'd already studied his cases so I knew background on each one already. Five minutes later, my arms were full of folders and I was ready to go home, pour some wine, slip on a tank top and sweatpants, and kick my feet up while reading through some of the most infamous of cases to ever hit New York City.

"I guess I should've been quicker," Chris said, as he walked up on me just as I was tossing the strap of my purse over my shoulder. "I got the scraps... ended up with the case he just lost yesterday. Everyone can tell you how he could have won that case... make sure that the damn witness shows up."

"I'll trade you," I blurted out and instantly wanted to take it back.

Wrinkling his brows at me, Chris peered at me curiously before dropping his attention to the files in my arms.

"Now why would you want to do that? You got first pick, right? You should have some good ones," he said, before reaching out to poke at one of the ones I was holding.

I balanced the files in my other arm on top of my chest, so I could use my hand to pull the one he was looking at and nudge it towards him.

"Here you go. State vs. Gotti. That's a good one."

Impressed by the trade, he handed over the file on Luke Murray and shrugged as if saying 'your loss'. To be honest, I was probably just as confused as he was. Luke Murray's case was an easy one and

Pelmington had lost it at no fault of his own. He'd queued everything up nicely and his witness didn't show up. It was obvious. But still... I felt the need to read more about the minor details that may not have been mentioned in court, including Luke's background. I knew he definitely had not graduated from anybody's college—unless 2 Chainz was running some university I didn't know about.

"Can I walk you out?" Chris said in a low tone, and I felt my tongue get heavy in my mouth, so I just nodded my head.

He smiled and grabbed a few of the folders out of my hand to provide me with some relief, and a warm feeling crept up in me as my heartbeat sped up in pace. I felt like a little girl in high school right after her crush offered to walk her to class and carry her books for the first time.

Chris was the type of guy that I always envisioned I'd end up with. He had a great background, shared my same passions, had suffered through the trials of growing up with a parent who had achieved wonders he could only hope he would... he understood me. And did I really have to mention the fact that he looked *identical* to Jesse Williams? Take Jesse Williams, swap the blue eyes for hazel ones, make him slightly taller and a half-shade darker, and you had Chris. He was *fine*.

"So what do you have planned for the weekend?" he asked, just as we walked outside. My eyes darted to the folders in my hands. "Besides going over the cases, I mean."

Twisting up my lips, I tried to ignore the stirring in my stomach and act normal.

"Uhm… I don't know. I guess catch up on a few episodes of *Scandal* and maybe read," I replied, giving an honest answer that I instantly regretted.

Shit, why didn't I just lie? What was so hot about watching *Scandal* and reading over the weekend? I knew I was lame but he didn't have to know. All of a sudden, I felt like my breath was getting caught up in my throat and I stopped walking for just a minute to catch my breath.

"Hey, you okay?" he inquired as he bent down to look me in my eyes.

His forehead was creased with concern as he ping-ponged his eyes back and forth between mine, searching for any indication that something was wrong.

"Your eyes are a little red. Have you had any water today?"

"No," I muttered breathlessly, and he nodded his head as his lips formed a line. He cradled the folders in one arm and reached into his laptop bag, pulling out a bottle of water.

"Here."

He opened it and held it to my lips so I could drink, and I slipped and fell right into lust. I gulped that water down like it was the magical elixir for eternal life. He could have been holding up a bottle of gasoline to my lips and I would have drank it down without a single question.

"Feel better?" he asked, and I nodded my head, still on an emotional high from being taken care of by such a beautiful man. He flashed me a smile, making me weak in the knees, and we shared a brief couple seconds of staring into each other's eyes.

Very brief.

About two seconds shy of Chris taking my breath away with his hazel eyes, Blondy walked out and interrupted the entire vibe that we had going on with her silky, sweet and *sickening* voice.

"Heyyyy, you guys!" she said, although it was obvious that she was only addressing Chris.

"Hey, Tatiana," Chris greeted her with a genuine smile, just as she turned to stand right in front of him with her back to me.

Like I wasn't even there. I felt my temperature begin to rise right along with my anger, and I had to pray to Jesus to stop me from snatching her up. Never had I wanted to fight a woman over a man in my life, and I wasn't about to let Blondy take me there.

Suddenly, I felt a prickly sensation on the back of my neck that I couldn't ignore, and my eyes began to scan the busy streets around me. My eyes stopped on a familiar figure that was all the way across the street from me, partially hidden by the droves of people walking on the sidewalk. I sucked in a breath and I finally realized how cruel life could be when my eyes locked in on Luke Murray. He was standing several yards away from where I stood, on the other side of the street, with his back on a pole and his arms crossed in front of his chest, staring right at me with that silly ass smirk on his face.

Oh God, I thought, my eyes darting to Blondy and Chris before looking back at the entrance to my job. What if someone saw him there looking at me?

Luke waved and I gasped, looking around to make sure no one saw him. Thankfully, everyone seemed to be minding their own business, completely uninterested in a 23-year-old Black woman who looked like she was losing her mind. Luke motioned with his hand for me to walk over to where he was, and I shook my head. But then, after seeing him shrug before taking a step forward like he was about to walk towards me, I took off before he did something that would derail my entire life.

"I gotta go!" I yelled at Chris, snatching my folders from his arms before I stormed away, across the street. "See you later!"

"Hey!" Chris called out from behind me, but I only ducked my head and got lost in the New York City crowd.

Making a sharp left, I headed directly to the subway, gripping the folders in front of me while praying that Luke decided to leave me alone. What was with him popping up everywhere I was all of a sudden? What did he want with me?

"Wassup, ma?" I heard a voice say from my side, and I didn't even have to look up to see who it was. Stopping, I swirled around on the balls of my feet and narrowed my eyes at him, holding the folders in front of my chest like a makeshift barrier between us.

"What are you doing here? What do you want with me?" I asked him, furious and scared all at the same time. I felt beads of sweat sprouting at my hairline, even though it was pretty cool outside.

Luke's eyes widened for a minute as he processed my question, and then he began to laugh, tossing his head back a bit as I continued to glare back at him.

"Listen, yo, I just left from paying a friend a visit. I got friends in high places, if you didn't know," he said in a way that made me think he was alluding to some possible corruption in the system I held so dear to my heart. Snorting, I turned around and continued down the stairs to the train, not wanting to fall into another debate with him.

"You must've forgot that I saw what you picked up this morning at the pharmacy. So I know you ain't think a nigga was checkin' for your square ass!" he shot out just as I began to walk away, and my mouth dropped open in shock but I overcame it, and in less than a second, I was ready to get all up in his ass.

"Square ass?! If you ain't checkin' for me, then why the hell you lookin' at my ass?" I asked, swirling around to look at him, my eyes blazing with anger.

With a frown, he walked slowly forward until he was only a step above me and then paused, his face breaking into his infamous smirk.

"I wasn't talkin' 'bout your ass, ma. I was callin' you a square," he explained, making me feel even more stupid, if that was even possible.

"Oh," I muttered, ducking my eyes.

"But…" He paused and I lifted my head just in time to see him place his finger under his chin while allowing his eyes to drop down to my backside. My breathing stalled and I felt a rush of moisture between my legs that shocked the hell out of me. Luke withdrew his focus from my body and brought his gaze back to my eyes and, finally, I was able to breathe again.

"Your ass is a'ight," he said with a slight nod. "It's nice. A little small for my taste but some niggas like chicks with yo' kinda booty."

Still thinking on how he said my ass was nice, I blushed deeply. Luke caught my reaction and a light chuckle escaped his lips, making me groan inwardly. My body was betraying my mind because I knew I wasn't attracted to him in the least. But then... why the hell did I blush?

"UGH!" I grumbled, whipping back around.

Why was I even worried about him to begin with? Who cares what he thought? I wasn't impressed by him and he was probably the last person I wanted to impress.

My legs were moving at top speed as I pressed on to the train, but Luke still managed to maintain his spot right at my side, even though he was walking with his normal stride.

"Why are you following me?"

"Why you followin' *me*, nigga?" he shot back without delay and I cringed at being called 'nigga'. Never in my life had anyone ever called me a 'nigga'. Not ever.

"Don't you have a car?"

"Why don't you mind your business?" he said, mimicking my words from earlier. He was such a child. Like an annoying little five year old.

I got to the train just as the doors open and I jumped on, breathing a sigh of relief that I was finally able to escape Luke for the second time that day. But my hopes were dashed to shit when I saw him get on right behind me. Grumbling under my breath, I pushed on to an empty seat towards the back and kept my head down, staring at the back of the files in my arm.

About five minutes after the train had started to move, I thought that Luke had finally decided to leave me alone until I heard his voice coming from right behind me.

"I saw you wit' that pretty boy. He's not your type," he whispered in my ear. Squeezing my thighs tightly together, I tried to ignore the effect his close proximity had on me.

Scoffing, I rolled my eyes dramatically before turning sideways to glance at him.

"How could you *possibly* know anything about my type?" I asked him, but he only sat back in his seat and pulled up the edges of his lips into a satisfied, know-it-all smirk.

Blowing out hot air, I rolled my eyes again and grabbed my phone so I could check the news. Hopefully he would understand that I wasn't in the mood to talk.

"Oh my God! Outlaw!" a female voice chimed, interrupting me in the middle of an article about Pelmington's surprising loss in court. Keeping my head low, I casted my eyes upwards to see what was going on.

The train had stopped and on sauntered a trio of women around my age, dressed in skintight clothing with faces full of makeup and bundles on top of bundles of weave. Each of them had smiles plastered across their face as they shot seductive looks somewhere behind me.

"Hey, wassup? Shit... y'all fine as fuck," Luke said from behind me and I groaned. Here we go again. I was stuck bearing witness to another meet up between Luke and a few of his fans.

"Can we ride with you?" one of the girls asked.

"Or on you?" another added under her breath, but I still caught it. Thirsty.

"Ain't room unless one of y'all sit on my lap. You down, thick red?" I'm assuming he asked the shorter light-skinned one with curly red weave. His response agitated me way more than it should have and I squeezed my eyes closed, willing the train to go.

Two more stops, I thought as the train took off, while the girls filed into the seats behind me. I kept my head down and tried to ignore the giggling from behind as we took off.

"Ow!" I snapped when one of them knocked me with her elbow, not even bothering to turn around and say 'excuse me'.

"You mind if I put my hands here?" Luke asked and I could practically hear the smirk on his face. "It's gon' be a bumpy ride."

"Yeah, baby. You can put your hands wherever you like," the chick replied, and I rolled my eyes at how she'd deepened her tone, trying her hardest to be sexy. It was seven o'clock and, although the sun was starting to go down, it was way too early to be tossing out thirst traps right out in public.

Narrowing my eyes, I fought to block out the noise behind me and started back reading the article. It was pretty interesting… gave an overview of the case and a brief background on the Murray brothers. Luke was the youngest of them all, which I knew. But what I didn't know was that he had *six* other brothers, one of whom was deceased. I thought my situation was crazy with me being one of four, but he had six other brothers. Insane.

"Oomph. Ooooohhh, Outlaw, that feels *sooo* good!" I heard the girl murmur from behind me and I totally forgot all about the article I was reading. My face began to get hot and I felt a familiar sensation rise up in my chest. It's anger and it's rolling through me like waves but I'm also frustrated because I don't completely understand why.

"You like that?" Luke asked in a low voice, just barely audible over the rumbling of the train.

"Mmhmm. Shiiiiit," she moaned. "Right there…Ooh."

Was he fingering her? Right on the damn train?

"Aye, you next?" I heard him say to one of her friends who quickly replied 'yes' in a voice that seemed to come from the back of her throat, as if she were turned on seeing her friend being pleased.

I can't take this shit, I thought, snatching up my bags as soon as the train began to come to a halt. I was out of here. I was getting off a whole stop early, which meant I had about four blocks to walk until I got to my stop, but I didn't care. After witnessing that whole ordeal on the train, I was utterly disgusted and couldn't stand to be around Luke another second.

Them Goody Two-Shoe Chicks.

Outlaw

"What got you cheesin' and shit like that, nigga? You on that shit Doc cooked up?" Cree asked me as he rolled up a blunt.

We were sittin' on Big Mama's front porch waiting for Yolo, Kane and Tank to show up. Every now and then, we would just sit and chill at her spot to let the new niggas who moved in her hood know that she was not to be fucked with. There had been plenty times I tried to move her ass out the hood she lived in, but she wasn't having that shit.

She reminded us all often that our granddaddy had built her house with his bare hands, and she wasn't laying her head anywhere else but the grave when the time came. I hated to hear her say that shit. The last thing I wanted to listen to her out her mouth was some shit about her lying in a grave.

"I ain't cheesin' 'bout shit. Just thinkin' 'bout this dumb ass chick I met a few days back," I told him. I leaned over to see what was taking him so damn long to roll the blunt.

"Dumb?" he repeated with a grunt. "It look like you feelin' her ass from where I'm sittin.'"

"Well, nigga, you need to get'cha ass up because the sun must be in yo' damn eyes," I joked, laughing at him. "Ain't feelin' her ass like that. She D.A. though… wouldn't be bad to have her on the team."

The thought had occurred to me a few times that it would be good having somebody on the inside to keep Pelmington off my ass. He was my nigga when he was gettin' the old heads off the streets about a year ago. He made the job easy for me and my brothers. But since then, his old white ass had decided that his primary mission was now to be a permanent pain in the ass. He was always trying to catch us in shit. I was starting to think it made his dick hard just thinkin' about locking one of us up. It wasn't gonna happen because we were too smart for that shit, but the fact that he was trying so hard bugged the shit out of me.

"Yeah, I might be able to use her ass," I thought aloud as I scratched at my jaw, thinking about Janelle. There had to be a reason I kept running into her ass. Maybe this was it.

"You be careful wit' that shit," Cree warned me, licking the blunt that he'd finally finished rolling up. "Them goody-two-shoe chicks will get a nigga locked up on some bogus shit. It's like they ass be itching to go snitch on some shit."

Cutting my eyes at Cree, I reached over and snatched the blunt out of his hand and grabbed the lighter off the table between us.

"I told you I ain't feelin' her ugly ass like that. She basic as fuck…"

"Basic, huh?" he teased, smirking as if he didn't believe me. "A'ight, nigga."

Janelle was basic. She ain't wear no weave, didn't do shit with her hair beyond tugging it into a bun, she wore stockings with them long ass church-usher skirts that she stayed in, and she barely had a chest and only a lil' hump of an ass. At least that's what it looked like, but I couldn't really tell with all them clothes she always had on. A nigga could barely sneak a look at anything because she dressed like she was about to leave work at the courthouse to go jump around and preach in somebody's pulpit.

The chicks I usually went for were model chicks... video vixen type chicks. They had banging bodies, hair and nails stayed done like it was a requirement to live. They shoe game was just as fly as mine, if not better, and they dressed fly to match. I couldn't be seen with a bitch if she wasn't fresh to death.

I squinted my eyes just as Tank rolled up in his brand new black Escalade, his rims glistening in the light of the setting sun. His whip was fiyah and I had to admit it, even though I preferred sports cars.

As soon as he got out the car, I knew some bullshit was about to follow. I could see it all over his face. Yolo pulled up just as Tank walked over to where we were, and he and Kane jumped out his car, running up the steps to the patio.

"Wassup, niggas?" Yolo greeted us, dapping me up before reaching out for the blunt. I took one last pull and handed it over.

"Ain't shit," I replied. "Tank, why you look all fucked up in the face, nigga?"

Tank flopped down on the seat next to me and dropped his face in his hands, rubbing over it one time as we all watched, wondering who the hell died to have him lookin' this damn stressed.

"I got a bitch tryna throw a baby on me, nigga," he said finally, before letting out a heavy exhale. "Faviola… chick at the club way back that did that trick with the Sprite can on twerk night."

There was a moment of silence as we all played the mental video we had stored in our minds of when Faviola did her trick with the Sprite can. It was right before I got locked up and if Tank hadn't stepped to her first, I would've been the one she was tryin' to pin a baby on. That trick was a muthafuckin' beast with the tricks that night. It was obvious her ass never went a day without doin' that Kegel shit.

"*Damn*, nigga, what that put you up to? Five kids?" I asked him and Tank dropped his head. Of all of us, Tank was the easiest to get along with and the one with the best game to make a chick peel off all her clothes. That shit worked too well because he stayed getting hoes pregnant.

"Seven, if this one mine."

"Shit… Yolo, pass him the blunt. He needs it. That nigga already got a gang of kids and another on the way? Damn. Let him smoke all that shit," Cree instructed, and Yolo didn't waste any time before handing it over.

Damn, I thought, then I looked out at his Escalade. "Aye, you let her ride in yo' front seat?"

Tank turned to me, crinkling up his face in confusion before falling out in laughter. Cree, Yolo and Kane did the same thing, but I just scratched my head as I looked at all of them. They might have thought I was crazy but the only niggas without jits were me and the one with no car.

"Outlaw, that's some stupid shit, yo," Tank said before leaning back to hit the weed. "Don't nobody but yo' crazy ass believe that a nigga can get a chick pregnant by lettin' her ride in the front seat."

"I gotta agree wit' him on that one, bruh," Yolo chimed in. "LaTrese ain't the only one that I let ride up front in the whip."

"Yeah, but wasn't she the first?" I asked him, nodding my head because I already knew the answer. "It's the *first* chick that you let ride up there who gets pregnant. Happens every time. That's why I don't let them sit they ass in my shit."

"Bogus," Kane laughed as he shook his head. "Yo' ass is crazy, yo."

"Okay, let's find out," I smirked, nodding my head before turning my attention back to Tank. "You let her ride up front in the new whip?"

A few seconds of silence passed before Tank finally let out a breath and nodded his head.

"Yeah… right when I got it. About a month and a half ago," he admitted.

"And now she pregnant," I said with a satisfied smile. "Now fuck all y'all niggas. I be knowin' my shit."

My stomach growled and I realized that I hadn't ate nothing since early that morning before heading out to meet up with some niggas to let them know I was back, which meant we were back to business as usual. Standing up, I grabbed my phone and turned it on. It exploded with text messages… all of them from random broads that I could barely remember, asking me to come through. I was willing to pop up on a few of them but not with an empty stomach.

"Big Mama cooked?" I asked, looking at Cree.

"Hell naw. Said we old enough to either cook or buy our own shit," he replied, and I knew he was using her exact words because that was exactly how she would say it.

"A'ight. I'm 'bout to head on out. I got shit to do."

"And hoes to see," Kane added, giving me a warning look. "You better slow down wit' dat shit, Luke. These tricks be on trap-a-nigga missions out here." He cut a look at Tank who somberly nodded his agreement.

"That's why I always stay strapped," I replied, winking at the both of them.

It was true. I didn't know about my brothers but, as for me, I wasn't running up in shit raw. I didn't give a fuck how good it looked. These hoes out here that I fucked with had all kinds of killers between their legs and I wasn't 'bout that shit. Look at the lil' square ass lawyer chick. Even she had some nasty shit goin' on. Hell naw. If she was burning, that was proof that it wasn't safe out in these streets.

Standing up, I stepped into the house so that I could say bye to Big Mama. When I walked in, I found her exactly where I expected to, right in her recliner in front of the TV, watching a recorded episode of Maury. She loved trash TV, although the only thing she'd do while watching was talk shit about how dumb the people were on the show.

"Aye, boy, what trouble you 'bout to get into?" she asked, as I leaned down to get a hug. She kissed me on my cheek and I pulled away.

"Not too much, Big Mama. Might find me a girl or two," I teased with a smile, knowing that she was about to get in my ass.

"You need to find *one* nice lil' girl so I can finally get me some great grands outta you before I go," she huffed while cutting me a side-eyed look. "I would like to see you happy and with a family before I head on."

Feeling my chest get tight, I shook my head. "I don't want to hear no more talk about you headin' on nowhere, Mama." She rolled her eyes but I was serious. "I'll holla at you in a few days. You cookin' on Sunday?"

"Hell naw!" she said and I fell out laughing. "And don't think I didn't feel the money you just slipped into my pocket. Boy, you not as smooth as them lil' girls out there got you thinkin' you is."

"I love you, Mama," I said, smiling at her as I walked back to the door.

"Love you too, Luke."

***

About fifteen minutes later, I was straight demolishing some hot wings from a spot owned by one of my homeboy's pops. In fact, that's what it was called: Pops. Pops had the best wings in Brooklyn, the only ones that reminded me of a few spots back home.

"Glad to see you back, Outlaw," Pops said, as I stuck a whole wing in my mouth as soon as he set the tray down in front of me. They were hot, greasy and smothered in sauce, just like I liked them.

"Yeah, they tried to hold me up but you know nothin' can keep a real nigga down," I told him.

"Mmhm," Briyana, his daughter, said from behind him. I shot

my eyes back to where she was standing and she blew me a kiss before licking her lips. Her ass was wild and had been feeling a nigga for a minute, but I wouldn't hit it. She was my boy's sister and I ain't even wanna cause no shit by making his sister fall in love with this dick.

"Naw, they can't. I knew you would pull through. They on ya ass though, from what I been readin' in the paper. Y'all just be smart and play it safe," Pops told me, totally oblivious of the fact that Briyana was behind him showing me her tits.

"A'ight, Pops," I said with a smirk on my face. "Aye, I gotta get out of here but I'll check in with you again soon."

"A'ight," he replied. He turned around just as Briyana turned to stick her titty back in her shirt. She was on some bogus shit.

Shaking my head, I walked out of the wing spot and decided to hit up the pharmacy to holla at my nigga, Tony. For some reason, Janelle was still on my mind and I wasn't sure why. Although she would be a good ally to have, I knew that wasn't the real reason. And it wasn't because I was feeling her too, because I wasn't. She just seemed like a cool chick, and I had to admit that it was funny as hell fucking with her.

The pharmacy was only half a block away, so I decided to walk over to it while I finished off my wings. I was used to walking anyways. Yeah, I was smart and, yeah, I had money, but I would forever be just a young nigga from the streets. Some shit you couldn't take out of people and that was one thing you couldn't take from me. I bought nice shit but I wasn't changed by that shit. I ain't have no issues with flat-footing it or taking the subway when it made sense. It was just how I was.

"Yo, Outlaw!" Dr. Mezianni greeted me as soon as I walked in the door.

Pulling the chicken wing from my mouth, I held out my hands and smiled.

"Wassup, nigga?! Where da hell was you at last night?" I asked him, referring to the poker game my brothers and I played every other Thursday, along with some cool ass muthafuckas in the neighborhood. Dr. Mezianni was one of them.

"Oh, we back on! We stopped playing after you left. Next time, I'll be there," he said and I nodded my head.

"Hell yeah, you will. I need them chips, nigga. I see you got some new employees up in this bitch... you must be gettin' ya cake up," I replied, looking behind him at a fine ass chick who had been working the drive-thru window. Her customer drove off and she turned around, smiling hard as hell when her eyes met mine.

"Oh, you mean Valerie?" Dr. Mezianni said, using his thumb to point behind him. "Yeah, she good. Smart too."

He wiggled his eyebrows and I couldn't help laughing at his crazy ass. He was always trying to match me up with some chick. Looking back at Valerie, I had to admit he had good taste though. Shawty was sexy. Even with the white lab coat on, I could see that she had a nice body up under her clothes. She was cute in the face too. Long hair, soft eyes, nice skin and white teeth... plus, from the way she kept checking a nigga out all bashful and shit, I could tell she was feeling me.

"A'ight," I nodded, licking my lips. "Tony back there?"

"Yeah, he's here," Mezianni said, grinning as he finished packaging up something. He winked and pushed it across the counter at me.

Nodding my head, I grabbed it and stuffed it in my pocket. Mezianni was always hooking me up with some shit for Yolo to whip up.

"Tony is in the back stocking up. I'll go get him."

As soon as Mezianni was out the way, I set my sights on the fine ass shawty behind him. She didn't know it yet but she was about to fall in love.

"Aye, Valerie…"

She gave me a smile with her brows bunched up in a frown.

"What'chu lookin' like dat for? That's your name, right?" I asked with a teasing smile. I licked my lips and watched as her eyes followed my tongue. She damn near stopped breathing. I had a crazy effect on women and it came without me really trying but it worked every time.

"Yeah… but my friends call me 'Val,'" she informed me, placing the papers she was holding down before walking over to stand in front of me.

"Well, can I call you 'baby'?" I know that line was lame as hell but I could tell she was the type of chick who thought 'lame' shit was cute. And I was right. She instantly started giggling, as she ducked her head and pushed a strand of her hair behind her ear.

"If you want to," she told me with a gentle shrug.

"Aye, can I get your number?" I asked, shoving my phone at her before she could answer. She hesitated for only half a second before grabbing it, putting her number in it and then handing it back to me.

"What you put it under?" I leaned over the counter, pushing my face closer to hers. She smelled good as hell. Like cinnamon or some sugary shit females wore because they knew niggas liked it.

"Val."

"Nigga, I told you I was gone call you 'baby'!" She giggled and I knew it was gonna be easy as hell to get in her pants. Just like I wanted. I ain't have time to be trying to convince a chick she wanted something both of us already knew she wanted.

"Aye, nigga, what's up?" Tony piped up, walking from the back.

"Ain't shit, bruh," I told him as I reached out to dap him up. "Real shit, I need a favor."

Tony nodded his head and reached out for the empty wing container in my hand then tossed it in the trash.

"Whatever it is, I got'chu," he said, and I glanced behind him at Val to make sure she wasn't paying attention.

"There was a black chick came in here the other day… got a prescription for some shit. I need her number." Tony stared at me with some dazed look in his eyes like he had no idea who the hell I was talking about and, for some reason, I started to get a little agitated as I continued trying to describe her.

"Bourgeois lookin' chick… lawyer. Remember, I was talking to her when I left out?"

"Oh yeah!" he said, finally. "Yeah… she had some shit with her. You know what I mean, right?" He gave me a wide-eyed look and I knew he was talking about the reason for the medication she'd been prescribed.

"She said it wasn't for her… that she got it for a friend," I explained, telling him exactly what Janelle had told me. He gave me a doubtful look and, I don't know why, but I started to get mad again.

"Nigga, just look her ass up in there and give me her number," I demanded roughly. A smirk rose up on the side of Tony's face and I had to look away to stop myself from choking his ass.

"I ain't tryin' to holla at her like that. So whatever she dealin' with ain't my problem," I felt the need to state.

"A'ight. Yo, it ain't my business anyways," he said before turning to key a few things into the computer.

Ya damn right.

Fighting the urge to say something, I looked behind him at Val at the same time that she glanced up at me. She was sexy but there was something about her that reminded me of every damn chick I met so beyond wanting to hit it, I wasn't interested at all.

"Here you go," Tony said, holding out a piece of paper at me. I grabbed it and tucked it in my pocket.

"Good lookin' out, nigga." I nodded my head at Tony before turning to walk out.

I was on some thirsty shit. Never in my muthafuckin' life have I had to get a chick's number in any other way than from her directly. This was some bullshit.

Childish.

Janelle

Pelmington gave us a week to go through all the case files and figure out a way to beat each case. But after working for only four days, I was done with all of them. Well, all of them except for the one on Luke Murray. Every time I looked at the picture in his file, I started thinking about that day on the train and got aggravated all over again. What kind of nasty ass dude fingers a girl in public and in broad daylight? Just sick.

I heard a door open and looked up just as Val walked out of her room with her wet hair wrapped up in a towel and another towel wrapped around her body. She seemed to be in a chipper mood and I was happy that she had finally found a way out of the funk she'd been in the past few days.

"What's got you so happy?" I asked, dropping the files on my lap. Val turned to me, her eyes growing dim as she hesitated before speaking. My heart dropped and I fought the urge to roll my eyes. It was obvious that this was about some new man she'd met.

"I'll tell you but don't judge me, okay?" she started, and I groaned inwardly.

"Okay," I muttered, not even trying to hide the annoyance in my tone. But Val didn't seem to care at all because in the next moment, she was sitting across from me with a big ass smile on her face, ready to dish all details on her new Mr. Right.

"So, I met a guy… at work. He's not my normal type but he has this vibe that I really like. Like, he's more of a roughneck type—" I rolled my eyes before I could stop myself. "—No! Roughneck in a good way—"Another eye roll. "—Janelle! You said you wouldn't judge."

Sighing, I nodded my head. "You're right. Go on," I told her as I began nibbling on the cap of my pen.

"Anyways, we've been texting back and forth since we met and now he's coming over to pick me up for a date…" She paused. "Well, not pick me up because I'm driving us but…"

"Sounds like a real winner," I said, my tone filled with sarcasm but she didn't even seem to catch it.

"He's just sexy as hell and he's friends with Tony so I know he's a good one. Tony told me all about him but he didn't even need to because right when I saw him, I was like 'damn, he could get it!'," she finished, laughing.

Blinking, I just stared at her. I know, I know. I was supposed to be the supportive friend who always fed bullshit to my friends regardless of the stupid things they do. The type of friend who said whatever it was that my girlfriend wanted me to say just so she didn't feel like she was being a hoe… or stupid… or whatever. That wasn't me. And, yes, I've heard that as an attorney, I need to be comfortable lying, but I'm not there yet. So sue me.

"All I have to say is, I'm not picking up no more prescriptions for your ass so you better keep your legs closed," I replied with a matter-of-fact tone that snatched the smile right off of Val's face.

"JANELLE!" she shrieked.

"What?! I'm just lettin' you know now before you—"

"It just *kills* you to be a friend, doesn't it?" Val snapped, jumping up from the couch. She stood in front of me with one hand on her hip and the other still holding onto her towel.

"Like, you can't just stop being a bitch long enough to actually be happy for somebody, huh? That's why you don't have any friends now!"

I flinched when she said that. Wow, now that hurt. But Val wasn't anywhere near finished.

"People don't want another mother, they want a friend who is going to stand by them and be supportive whether they are right or wrong. The type of friend who is going to stand back and let them make their own decisions but still be that shoulder to cry on when they need one. I thought you'd be that! The one who would help me roll up on a nigga and slash his tires or something if he fucks me over—"

"But destroying someone's property is a crime. We could go to—"

"UGH!" Val groaned, cutting me off. Then she whipped around and stomping off to her room, leaving me utterly confused. Who wanted a friend who would just lie to them all the time? Not me.

Sighing, I went back to my files but I couldn't focus so I reached over and picked up my phone, turning it on for the first time that day. Immediately, my phone began to chime with messages and I frowned, wondering who it was. Like Val had so easily pointed out, I didn't have many friends so it had to be family.

The first text was from my father telling me he loved me. That made me smile. The next was from my sister, Carmella, but the last one… it came from a number I didn't recognize.

What you doing? was all it said. Creepy.

Who is this? I replied back, frowning as I bit down on my lip. I waited for what felt like forever and then finally I got a response.

Who you think it is? There was also a smiley face emoji.

After reading it over a few times, I began to smile as well. This was obviously Chris texting me from his work phone, trying to throw me off. He was the only person I could think of who would bother messaging me. Shifting to get comfortable, I became totally lost in my phone as we began to text each other back and forth.

Me: I'm reading over case files.

Him: Sounds boring.

Laughing, I shook my head.

Me: Well, what are you doing?

Him: Getting ready for a date.

My smile dropped instantly and I tried to ignore the pang in my chest. There was the confirmation. Chris was going out with Blondy. So as much as I thought that we could one day make a connection, it was obvious that he only saw me as a friend. I didn't know how to respond so I paused and another message popped up.

Him: Would rather be taking you out though.

The smile was back and so were the flutters in my stomach. I was acting like such a girl and I hated it but loved it at the same time.

Me: I would rather that too.

Him: Want me to pick you up?

YES! Is what I wanted to scream but I was able to hold on to my joy just a bit longer to peck out a response.

Me: You're going to cancel on Tatiana?

I had to ask just to be clear because there was no way I was going on any three party dates with him and Blondy again. It was sickening and my stomach couldn't take it anymore.

Him: Who?

I frowned as I looked at the message. What did he mean who? Was he going out with someone other than Blondy? Shit… I had more competition than I thought. Before I could respond, another text came through.

Him: Wait… who the fuck do you think this is?

Okay. Now I was really confused and the creepy feeling started to come back.

Me: Chris. This isn't Chris?

I saw the read receipt come through showing that whoever it was on the other side had read my message and I waited for another response to come through. The longer I had to wait, the more panicked I became. Who the hell had I been messaging all this time? Finally, after what felt like forever, a text finally appeared.

No, Janelle.

Oh. My. God.

Me: Well, who is this???

I stared at my phone waiting for a response for over fifteen minutes but none came. Finally, I decided to just call the number, but I was sent to voicemail after the first ring. I sent out a series of messages, all of them demanding that whoever it was on the other end tell me how they got my number and who they were, but none of the messages were read or responded to. Eventually, I just blocked the number and decided to jump in the shower to wash the creeped out feeling away.

Val was in her room blasting music by the time I got in the shower, and I knew that she was doing it to annoy me since she thought I was trying to study. This kinda shit was the reason I didn't have a lot of friends, but with three other sisters, I didn't need friends anyways.

As soon as the water hit my body, I began to relax and clear my mind. Val came and banged on the door, yelling something that I couldn't hear but I figured she was just telling me she was leaving. 'Bout damn time.

The water had begun to get cold, so I stayed in for about a few minutes longer before turning it off so I could get out and enjoy having the place to myself. I was already getting excited about the prospect of being alone in front of the TV with a glass of wine as I caught up on some TV series that I loved. Or, I might even be a little adventurous and try out some of the Apple Crown Val had bought when she was dating the Netflix and Chill guy.

With my excitement building up steadily inside me, I wrapped the towel around my wet body and opened the door so I could walk to my room and finish getting dressed. As soon as the door swung open, I sensed a figure sitting in the living room and I stopped in my tracks, stunned as I gripped the door handle. My eyes shot over to see what it was, and they connected with the face of the last person that I expected to see sitting in my living room, with his hair braided to perfection, dressed like something straight out of the hood star version of GQ Magazine.

"Aye… Blackbone," Luke said, looking directly at me. A smirk slid up the edge of his lips and I gasped.

And I dropped my towel.

"Damn." His eyes were wide as they raked quickly over my naked body before I was able to reach down and grab it up. But I moved so quickly that my wet foot slipped on the moist tile and I twisted around, giving him an eyeful of my ass right before I fell on it.

"Umph!"

"Daaaaammmn," he commentated and I heard the delight in his voice at the same moment that I felt the heat in my cheeks. This moment couldn't possibly get worst.

Scrambling, I grabbed the towel and slid back in the bathroom, slamming the door closed. My heart was beating so hard in my chest, it muted out all sound as I sat on the tile floor, gripping the towel that had failed me in my hand while trying not to die from sheer embarrassment. In the middle of convincing myself that things could have been worse—although I don't know exactly *how*—my thoughts were interrupted by someone tapping on the door.

"Aye, you might as well come out of there. I done see everything already…"

"Oh God," I muttered, dropping my face into my palms.

75

"…and when I say everything. I mean *everything*. Who knew you was holdin' like that. I mean, it ain't big or no shit like that but you got a lil' hump back there," he continued, whispering through the door. "That's enough meat for a nigga to twerk wit', ya feel me?"

Is it possible to die from embarrassment?

After deciding that it was time to put my game face on and stop wallowing in my shame on the bathroom floor, I wrapped the towel around my body and stood up. Taking a deep breath, I let it out slowly then opened up the door... to find Luke leaning back against the wall ahead of me with his arms crossed in front of his chest and that stupid smirk on his face. God, I hated it and I hated him even more.

"What are you doing here?" I hissed at him with a deep frown on my face.

"Takin' a chick out. I told you I was gettin' ready for a date."

It took me a second but when I finally figured it out, I felt a wave of relief ripple through me. So he'd been the one texting me. Wait... but why was I relieved? That wasn't a good thing.

"Oh, I forgot... you thought you were textin' pretty boy," he scoffed, and for some reason I felt a flare of guilt wash through me. "I told you he wasn't your type. But whatever."

"Oh, but Val's *your* type?" I shot back, making sure to keep my voice low. Luke shrugged, keeping the humor shining in his eyes.

"Why? You jealous?"

My cheeks got hot to the point that they stung. He had picked up on an emotion I wasn't really ready to admit that I'd noticed in myself.

It was like he was easily able to pick up on my inner-thoughts and that frustrated me.

"Jealous?!" I repeated, my voice much louder than I'd intended it to be. "Why would I be jealous that she's going out with *you*? You're disgusting, rude, 'ignant', you dress like you're part of an elementary rapper's entourage, you have nasty tattoos all over your body and let's *not* forget your yuck mouth!"

Luke's eyes narrowed into slits and his upper lip twisted into a snarl, reminiscent of the one I'd seen on his face that day in court.

"Yuck mouth?" he repeated. "What kind of shit is that to say to a nigga?" I almost began to shake as his anger radiated off of him and swarmed around me. Then, all of a sudden, he relaxed his face and the smirk came back to his lips, although his eyes still maintained their flame.

"Yeah... I guess Val is my type. She looks good, smells good, dresses good. She got a banging ass body, she ain't taking prescriptions for a yucky coochie—" I snorted, almost unable to stop myself from correcting him. "—And most importantly, she isn't runnin' around droolin' over a pretty boy who don't want nothin' to do with her black ass!"

I felt tears of fury come to my eyes but I fought them away. How *dare* he act like he knew all about my life only after a matter of days? Ugh, I swear I couldn't stand him!

Sneering at Luke, I gripped the towel tightly in my hands and pushed past him as we glared at one another. Then just as I got to my room door, feeling like I just had to do something to further indicate just how angry I was, I twisted around and flipped him a bird before stomping inside and slamming the door behind me.

Childish… I know. But he acted so much like a fuckin' kid that he brought the same thing out of me.

***

After hearing Luke and Val leave, it took me a while to regain my concentration enough so that I could focus back on the files. The sound of Val's voice as she giggled like Luke was the funniest man on Earth, annoyed the hell out of me. She was even worse than Blondy. It was sickening. What about a man made a woman act so fuckin' dumb?

After writing up my thoughts on how the cases I reviewed could have been won, I was left with the last one. The one that I regretted even taking in the first place. Luke's.

"Ugh… can't stand his ass," I grumbled as I tossed the folder open and began pulling out the papers inside. My hand landed on a photo of Luke when he was initially arrested. He looked just like he did the few times I'd seen him… complete with the fire in his eyes. Pulling it close, I scrutinized every detail about him.

He wasn't that bad looking besides all of the tattoos on his neck. Okay… if I were being honest, I would have to admit that I actually considered him to be attractive but I would never, ever let him know that. He had really nice skin with bedroom eyes… the kind that made you feel warm inside whenever he looked at you. I'm sure it was a fact he was well aware of being that I'd seen him trying to use them to his advantage plenty of times when he was throwing game on his lil' female fans.

I pulled out another photo, this one a shot of his entire body. He was covered with tattoos, donning an entire sleeve on both arms and all up his neck. But that's where they stopped. He didn't have a single one on his face. His hair was long and smooth with a hint of a curl. In the picture, he didn't have it braided back in a nice style. Instead, his hair hung widely around his head, creating a halo that hung low over his shoulders.

Pushing the pictures aside, I grabbed up a transcript of Jamal's initial testimony and began reading it. Although I'd heard Pelmington question him in court, I knew that he'd cherry-picked which questions to ask in order to win his case. I wanted to know everything that Jamal had said about Luke's crimes right in the beginning.

Pelmington: Do you know Luke Murray?

Jamal: Who?

Pelmington: You might refer to him as Outlaw.

Jamal: Oh…Yes.

Pelmington: How do you know him?

Jamal: He's one of the Murray brothers… We kinda grew up together.

Pelmington: And during that time, have you seen them commit any crimes?

Jamal: Yes. Lots of 'em.

Pelmington: Including Luke?

Jamal: Hell yeah! He's the worst of 'em all. Outlaw's done a lot of shit but he's smart so he get away wit' it.

Pelmington: Like killing Torian Green?

Jamal: Uh… yeah, but that nigga deserved the shit, for real.

Pelmington: Why do you say that?

Jamal: Because Torian had raped our homegirl; left her bleedin' out her ass and all. It was a chick we all grew up wit'. He raped her and left her bloody and shit in the middle of the fuckin' street. It took three days for her to talk but when she did… Outlaw handled it. ASAP.

Grimacing, I pulled my eyes away from the transcripts as a funny feeling fell over me. Being that I was the daughter of an attorney who was a firm upholder of the law, I never doubted anything pertaining to justice and I had a strong belief in things being either right or wrong. And I've definitely never felt any kind of mercy for anyone being prosecuted for killing someone.

But still… something about the transcripts made me think of Luke differently. If something so horrific had happened to me, as what happened to his friend, my father probably wouldn't have hesitated to do the same thing. And he was the most upstanding person I knew.

After a few seconds of meditating on my personal opinion about Luke's actions, I shook my head and pushed the thoughts away. I was an attorney specializing in criminal law. A prosecuting attorney. That meant that my personal feelings about something didn't matter. It was all about getting justice for the victim and, regardless to what Luke's reasons were, he should have left it up to the courts to decide what to do about Torian rather than taking matters into his own hands. He was guilty and deserved to be punished for his crimes. Right?

Reaching down, I picked back up the picture of Luke and stared at it. As much as I tried to convince myself that he deserved to spend a lifetime in prison for his crimes, something in the pit of my stomach said otherwise.

With a sigh, I looked up and my eyes focused on the clock. It was almost two o'clock in the morning and Val still wasn't home. They'd been gone for hours. What could her and Luke possibly be doing at two in the morning? I felt myself begin to feel jealous of Val for the first time since I met her and it made me pause. Glancing back at Luke's photo, I scrutinized him a little longer, trying to find an answer for the way I was feeling.

About an hour later, I was still reading over the details of Luke's case, every page telling me more and more about his brothers and the many crimes they were suspected of. From what I read, they'd had a hand in every major robbery in New York City, but all of the evidence the district attorney's office had been able to collect was circumstantial at best. There were never any witnesses or any hard evidence.

Matter of fact, the few things that Pelmington had been able to scrape together on them was so ridiculous that it almost seemed like the Murray brothers were taunting the detectives investigating their crimes. There would be things like a video clip of Luke or one of his brothers standing in plain sight in front of a bank, ordering food from a food truck, only minutes before a bank nearby was robbed. Or, my personal favorite, a photo of Luke flipping off a camera down the street from a major jewelry store that had been hit as soon as a shipment came in of many high priced diamonds. But there was never anything else to pin them to any of the robberies. If they had actually done these crimes, they weren't amateurs in the least.

Finally, I got to the last sheet of paper. A full bio of Luke 'Outlaw' Murray. I skimmed it quickly, noticing that he was born in late May.

A Gemini, I thought, pausing. That explained why he was crazy as hell one minute and then cool as a fan the next. His ass shifted so fast through personalities, it was insane.

He was from Miami, Florida... which explained the deep southern accent and the flashy way he dressed. My eyes continued to scan through the bio but I froze suddenly when they landed on something else.

Education: Luke Murray graduated from University of Miami with a degree in Engineering before obtaining a master's degree in IT from New York University. Per his transcripts, he scored very highly in every subject and is very skilled when it comes to systems.

"What?!" I said, squinting hard at the paper as I clutched it tightly in my hand. I read the paragraph over once again and finished just as I heard someone unlocking the door.

Stuffing the papers back into the file, I looked up just as the front door opened and Val walked in... with Luke right behind her.

"Shit! Oh... hey, Janelle. I thought you would have been asleep by now." An uneasy expression crossed Val's face and I knew right then that she'd actually hoped I was asleep.

"No, just trying to get some work done," I told her, and she nodded her head before closing the front door.

"Okay, well... I'll see you in the morning," she muttered and turned to walk away, holding Luke by his hand as she led him to her room.

My eyes swooped over to Luke, unable to ignore his heated stare. He was giving me a taunting smile, as if he were trying to rub it in my face that he was about to join Val for a nightcap. Lifting his free hand, he wiggled his fingers at me, giving me a teasing wave as he stomped behind her. Scoffing, I rolled my eyes and looked away. They walked down the hall and the door closed to Val's room, at the same moment that I became acutely aware of my heart thumping hard in my chest.

"Can't stand him," I muttered, folding my arms in front of my chest. I was painfully aware that, once again, he had me acting like a child.

The door opened again and out walked Luke. Seething, I followed his movements as he emerged from the hall and walked right into the kitchen, opening the refrigerator like he owned the place. Rolling my eyes, I snatched up my files and got up, heading straight to my room.

"Why you mad for?" he asked, just as I approached where he stood in the kitchen. I stopped and he walked out, standing right in front of me as he sipped from a bottle of water with a sickening smile on his face. He had that same glimmer in his eyes that was always there when I felt like he was laughing at me on the inside. I don't know why he thought my misery was so damn hilarious.

"I'm not mad," I shot back, matter-of-factly.

"No? I just thought for a minute you was feelin' some type of way 'cause Val's 'bout to get this dick."

I sucked in a sharp breath and almost dropped the files from my arms. Watching my reaction, he began to chuckle as he sipped his drink, his eyes never leaving mine.

"I don't care what you're about to give her," I sniffed, gritting my teeth to keep a straight face. "And shouldn't you be in there with her instead of annoying me?"

He shrugged. "She asked me to step out so she could get things right for a nigga… slip into some sexy shit, I guess."

As if on cue, I heard Val turn on the radio and I felt myself cringe.

"Whatever," I grumbled, starting back towards my room.

"Aye, it could've been you," he said from behind me. "But you wanna play hard wit' a nigga."

"Oh, but I'm not your type," I couldn't resist saying as I turned around and shrugged. "Right?"

He wet his lips, letting his eyes fall over my body in a slow, seductive fashion that set my soul on fire. Then he came back up, making sure to follow every single one of my curves before finally meeting my gaze.

"Yeah… you right." He smirked and finished off the last of his water while keeping his eyes on me. "Naw, you ain't my normal type."

"Ugh!" I huffed and pushed into my room, pressing the door closed behind me. He annoyed me but I was more frustrated at myself at the moment.

As repulsive as I tried to tell myself he was, he had an effect on me that I couldn't explain. And the way that he looked at me… it made me feel absolutely naked and raw.

Well…, I thought as I looked down at what I had on and realized that I nearly was naked.

I was in the stuff I wore around the house: thin little satin shorts and a tank top. I was covered but I didn't leave much to the imagination. Not like he had to imagine much anyways. I'd shown him every damn thing fresh out the shower.

"Luke? Heyyy," I heard Val say, walking out of her room. "You ready?"

"Luke, heeeyyyyy. You reaaady?" I mimicked her annoying voice while twisting up my face. Grabbing my iPod, I pushed the headphones in my ear and fell down onto the bed, staring at the ceiling.

I really didn't even understand why I was so bothered by what they were doing or why I felt like I couldn't stand Val in that moment. Maybe it was because I was tired of her bringing over these random ass men and fuckin' them on the first night. It definitely didn't have a thing to do with Luke so that had to be the reason why.

Yeah… Luke definitely wasn't the reason why.

Changing Faces.

Janelle

*A*fter a long night of tossing and turning, I woke up to the sound of my phone buzzing against my face.

"Hello?"

"Hey, sisterrrrrrrr!"

"Hey, Carmella," I groaned, sitting up in the bed. Reaching out, I grabbed the alarm clock next to me and looked at it. Six o'clock in the morning. What was Carmella even doing awake? She was more of a noon riser.

"Guess what?" she chimed on and I grunted.

"Mel, it's too early to guess. Just tell me."

"Well… I'm in New York! Just got off the plane. Send me your address and I'll grab a cab," she continued, squealing into the phone.

The thought of having my sister in the city instantly brought a smile to my face. Although Carmella was always convincing me to do things I would have never considered doing during her visits, I always ended up having fun no matter how much I groaned about it in the beginning.

"I'll send it to you when we get off the phone. You know I have to work today, right?"

"You always have to work, Jani. I'll catch up with you after work.

I have some friends I'm going to meet up with while you're busy," she informed me and I shook my head. Carmella always had friends. No matter where she went, she always managed to find someone to hang out with.

After hanging up the phone with her, I texted her the address to the apartment and let her know I'd leave a key under the doormat. Then it was time for me to get up and get ready for work. I was a little early but it was good because it gave me time to stop for coffee.

Once I'd showered and got dressed, I crept out of my room and down the hall, hoping that I wouldn't run into Val but when I got to the kitchen, I discovered that she was already up and about.

"Good morning," she said to me, her voice only above a whisper.

"Morning. Why are you whispering? You still have company?" I asked, my tone flat as I pushed by her to the fridge to load up on some water.

"No," she replied with her head down.

"Humph," I grunted, rolling my eyes. I saw her looking at me out of my peripheral but I didn't say anything because, for some reason, her presence was annoying me.

"I'll see you later. Oh, Carmella will be here later on," I grumbled as I walked by her once again, heading to the door.

"Janelle!" she called out just as I was about to leave and I stopped, cursing under my breath at having to stay for a second longer. The room had all of a sudden gotten too crowded.

"Huh?" I replied, with a little too much attitude. I turned around and squared my focus on her, struggling to keep my face neutral.

"I just wanted to say that you were right. I'm going to take a break and not date for a while," she admitted, shrugging her shoulders.

Okay, now I was curious. And a little happy about the fact that it seemed like her and Luke didn't work out. My mood shifted instantly.

"Oh... he didn't work out?" I asked her, trying to hide the many emotions that I was feeling at the moment. The main one being relief. I didn't want to admit it, but hearing that her and Luke may have not worked out made my attitude do a complete 180. But why? I couldn't even begin to explain why I felt so happy about it but I just did.

"No, it didn't. I tried to have sex with him... And I'm ashamed to say that I did after just getting over my other problem. But he wasn't into it. In fact, after you went to bed, he came in and told me some line about how I was a nice chick and all but he didn't want to try nothing with me. Then he left."

Wow, I thought. I was at a loss for words. I just stood there, dumbfounded, until I realized that she was waiting for me to reply. Clearing my throat, I said the first thing that came to mind.

"Val, it may be a good thing. Take some time off from men and focus on finishing school."

She nodded her head but the expression on her face was still so sad. She looked like a cute little puppy and I couldn't help but want to make her better.

"Tonight, I'm sure Carmella's going to drag me out to a club. Why don't you come with us?"

I didn't know it but those were the magic words. A light shined bright in Val's eyes and she smiled.

"Thank you! I can't wait!"

Pressing my lips together, I smiled back at her and then turned to leave. The cool air hit me as soon as I stepped out of the door and it was refreshing to finally be coming into winter.

I was walking down the sidewalk, heading to the coffee shop on the corner, when a fiery red Camaro rolled up on me really slow. Alarmed, I was about to speed up my pace when I saw that it was Luke. My heart jumped and I felt butterflies in my stomach. Surprisingly to me, a smile even began to tickle the corner of my lips when I saw that he was staring right at me. I stopped walking and he put the car in park before jumping out.

"You following me again?" I asked him, teasing as I ignored the feeling in the pit of my stomach. Something had changed. But after spending a whole night trying to ignore the fact that I was pissed about him having sex with Val, seeing him after learning that he hadn't done anything with her made me look at him a different way.

"This time I am," he admitted, and I felt a quiver run down my spine. "I texted and called you a few times. You takin' this stubborn shit too far. You can't text a nigga back?"

Confused, I frowned as I looked at him. His eyes were narrowed but he was only mildly angry. He seemed more annoyed than anything.

"I—I blocked the number."

"What?!" he snapped. "You *blocked* me? Damn."

Seeming irritated, he shook his head and I felt myself begin to panic when he started to walk away.

"No! I blocked the number before I realized it was you. After I kept asking who it was and didn't get a response," I admitted, licking my lips. "I'll unblock it now."

Pulling out my phone, I did just that as he watched me the entire time. Lifting my hand, I showed him the screen and a smile slowly eased up on his face then he nodded his head.

"Cool."

The wind blew hard around us as we stood staring at each other but I didn't feel the cold one bit. My insides felt warm and I had a bad case of the nervous jitters.

"So… you were waiting for me out here?" I asked, lifting one brow with my question.

"Naw," he replied, running his hand over his facial hair. "My grandmother actually lives a few blocks up. I spent the night with her. I just decided to pull through and saw you walking. Where you headed?"

"To get coffee," I told him, glancing towards the shop at the corner.

"Can I come with you?" he asked. The way he asked the question was odd. I could tell he wasn't used to asking for anything and now that he had, he was on edge about how I would respond. To my astonishment, I found myself nodding my head.

Shit! What was I doing? This was terrible and there were so many reasons why I couldn't be seen with Luke but… at the moment, I couldn't remember one. Not a single one. Damn it.

"Okay, give me a minute," he said and turned back to his car. Opening the door, he turned it off, grabbed his keys and then turned back to me.

"Let's go."

"Wait… you're going to leave your car right there?" I asked him, pointing to how he pulled it over in a 'no parking' zone.

He glanced from me to the car and then back to me before laughing a little. The sound sent a sexual wave through me that went right to the spot between my legs.

"This is Brooklyn…" he said like I was supposed to know what that meant. When I continued giving him a clueless expression, he continued on.

"I own this city. You ain't kno'?" He smiled and I snorted out a laugh, shaking my head.

"Actually, no. I wasn't aware," I replied honestly, shrugging lightly.

"You gon' find out."

I was caught off guard by that statement but even more so by the piercing stare that followed, so I turned and began to walk towards the coffee shop with him right beside me.

"You had coffee at this spot before?" he asked, breaking the silence.

Happy about the change in topic, I nodded my head.

"Yes, I actually go here for coffee whenever I get a chance. I found it right when we moved in the neighborhood about two months ago. It's the best coffee ever," I told him, rattling on as if I was the spokesperson for the place.

"That's what's up," was all he said.

When we got to the shop, he held his hand out to stop me when I was about to open the door and I looked at him confused.

"I got that," he said and then reached out and grabbed the handle, backing away so I could walk through.

"So sweet," I said in a teasing tone, although I was sincerely impressed.

"Don't get used to this shit," he shot back with a smile. He was always ready with his own slick ass response.

"OUTLAW! My dude, what's up, man?"

"Wassup, Jay C," Luke said, walking up from behind me. I stepped back and watched him dap up the guy behind the counter who barely said more than a few words to me although I came in every other morning.

"I heard you was back on the bricks, man. They couldn't keep a real one down for long, huh?" Jay C continued.

"Never that, nigga. They tried that shit tho'. I can't wait until they get tired of my ass and move on to some niggas worth trackin'."

"Fuck Pelmington. That muthafucka act like he ain't got shit else to do than be on yo' ass. He need to go back to focusin' on lockin' up them corporate white boys instead of fuckin' around with y'all Murrays. Y'all ain't done shit but steal from the rich and give to the poor. The real Robin Hood. Don't them muthafuckas celebrate that nigga?"

"Hell yeah," Luke replied, laughing. "Got movies 'bout his ass and all."

"See?" Jay C continued with his brows raised. "That proves they don't know shit."

Luke glanced in my direction but I dropped my head, feeling a little put off about the fact that I realized I lived in a neighborhood surrounded by people who loved him and would hate me, if they knew what I did and who I worked for. Thank God I wasn't wearing my badge. I'd learned from my run-in with Luke at the pharmacy to keep it in my purse until I actually got to work.

"Aye," Luke said and I felt his hand at my back, pulling me forward. "She came in here to grab some coffee."

Walking to the counter, I cleared my throat and looked up at Jay C to give him my order.

"I already know. You want a medium coffee, French Vanilla creamer and three pumps of sugar, right?"

I nodded my head before reaching down to fumble around in my purse for my wallet. As soon as I grabbed it, I reached out to hand Jay C a five-dollar bill but he shook his head.

"I can't take your money. If you're a friend of Outlaw's, you're a friend of mine. He gave my moms the money to start this spot. From now on, whatever you want is on the house," Jay C told me before turning to make my coffee.

Cutting my eyes to Luke, I saw that he had a wide grin on his face. Almost like he was gloating.

"So now you see a nigga ain't as bad as you thought, huh?" he teased, and I felt myself began to blush. Still, I played hard. I didn't want him to know that I was actually impressed.

"You're nice… but you ain't all that," I shrugged as I mocked his tone. The same one he used when he was telling me that my ass was 'a'ight' to be so flat, or letting me know that I was cool but not his type. He caught the playfulness in my tone and began to laugh.

"You crazy, yo."

After grabbing my coffee, I sipped quietly while Luke and Jay C said a few words. I was going to be late for work but, for some reason, I didn't care. I was curious about Luke, who seemed to be celebrated in the community. My father had told me stories about how the thugs where he stayed in the projects of Atlanta had terrorized the neighborhood, committing crimes and selling drugs. But Luke didn't seem to be like that. The people in the hood didn't fear him, they loved him. Maybe my daddy ain't know everything.

"You good?" he asked me as we walked out of the shop. I nodded my head, my mind still ruminating over how he was knocking down all of my stereotypes that I'd had about men who looked like him and found themselves on the bad side of the law.

"Everyone loves you here," I told him, thinking through my thoughts aloud.

"I told you this is my city," he replied with a tacit nod and smile. He stuffed his hands in his pockets and I followed behind him, walking in the complete opposite direction from where I needed to go.

"So what about all of the things you've done? All of the things that Jamal Shumpert was going to testify about?" I pressed on, curious about everything concerning him.

Luke was quiet for a minute and I wondered if he was going to answer me or not. He probably was selecting his words carefully. After all, I was part of Pelmington's team. How much could he really trust me?

"If you grew up here, you'd understand that shit ain't so black and white. You probably come from a place where the law is everything and that's where you place your trust. But in the hood, we play by goon rules. The law you love ain't worth shit 'round here," he finished, kicking at some gravel on the sidewalk.

He glanced at me, looking right into my eyes, and I saw that all of the silliness and teasing had passed away as he revealed his honest thoughts. It probably was at this moment that I realized that things would never be the same for me. For some reason, I kept running into Luke and, even though I didn't completely know why, I was beginning to see that it wasn't by accident.

After spending twenty-three years of my life waiting for the day that I could finally correct all that was wrong in black neighborhoods, by tossing the lawbreakers who resided there in prison, I was confronted by one in particular who didn't fit the mold that I'd constructed based on my father's experiences.

Luke was gritty, rude, street, was said to have little to no regard for human life and absolutely no regard for the law, but I was starting to see that there was another side to him. He sincerely cared about his community and the people in it. He wasn't a bad person even though he did 'bad' things. And even still... for the so-called 'bad' things he did, it seemed he had a good reason for them that went back to helping the people around him. He blew my mind. I had to know more about him.

"So, what makes a guy with an engineering degree from the University of Miami want to cover himself in tattoos and get a mouth full of gold teeth?" I asked, giving him a smirk of my own.

Luke stopped walking and smiled. That's when I realized we'd walked all the way back to his car. Leaning back on it, he crossed his arms in front of his chest and kept his eyes pinned on me.

"Because I like gold and I like tats," he replied with ease. "The only reason I don't put no shit up here is cuz my Big Mama told me not to cover up my handsome face." He shot me a look and I rolled my eyes. He was so cocky, it was ridiculous but cute at the same time.

"Hey... them her words, not mine."

There was twinkle in his eyes as he looked at me and it made me feel warm inside. I had a feeling that I would be just fine standing there and talking to him all day long but I had to get to work. I glanced at my watch and cringed. Shit. I was going to be late.

"You got somewhere to go?" he asked and I nodded my head.

"Yeah, I'm going to be late to the train," I sighed, and pulled my purse strap higher up on my shoulder as I started to walk away.

"Let me give you a ride," he offered and my stomach flip-flopped. I felt my cheeks heat up when the vision that immediately came to mind had everything to do with me riding something that was *not* his car.

"Okay," I replied as I shook the image away. Then I paused, wondering why I had just agreed to jump in the car with the man who had been prosecuted by my boss. This could end up very badly for me if anyone found out that I was on talking terms with Luke Murray. Like *extremely* bad.

"You comin' or not? Shit, I ain't got all day," Luke spoke up, cocking his head to the side as he ogled me.

Nodding my head, I pressed my lips together and walked forward. He opened the door and pulled up the passenger seat before turning to me. And that's when I stopped and frowned at him.

"What you doing?" I asked him, frowning from the car to him as he held the door open so I could slide into the back. "You want me to sit in the back seat?"

"Yeah. You don't like for a nigga to chauffeur you around?" he asked, looking at me like I was wrong for being ready to smack his ass.

"Oh, I'm not good enough to sit in your front seat?" I asked him and placed my hand on my hip.

Crinkling his brows, he pressed his lips firmly together and looked off into the distance before bringing his eyes back to me.

"It ain't like that, ma. Just get in," he told me nudging his head towards the car.

"Naw, I'm good."

Turning on my heels, I took off in the direction towards the train. I was mad as hell. What kind of man asks to take you somewhere and then tells you that you have to sit in the back? He tried to play it off by saying that chauffeur shit but I wasn't buying it.

"Shit!" I heard Luke curse from behind me as I pressed on, eager not to even glance in his direction. Seconds later, I heard the sound of feet running up behind me.

"My bad," he said, jumping in front of me to block my path. Rolling my eyes, I folded my arms in front of my chest and glared at him.

"I just don't like to…" he paused and I raised a brow, ready for him to continue.

But instead, he bit down on his bottom lip and glanced away, his eyes looking at nothing in particular as he battled the thoughts in his mind. Finally, he shook his head and turned back to me. His stare ran over me, starting from the bottom before he slid them upwards, completely throwing me off my game. My lips parted as I watched him, my sexuality incensed by the longing gaze in his eyes.

"Never mind," he muttered finally. "Come back. Let me take you where you need to go."

And with that he turned around, leaving me standing in the middle of the sidewalk feeling like I'd just experienced the best kind of foreplay even though he hadn't touched one part of me. If he could do all that with only his eyes, what could he do with his—shit. Did I really just think that?

By the time I turned around, Luke was already standing at his car with the front seat pushed back so I could sit down. Clearing my throat, I ignored the moisture between my legs and walked over, catching a whiff of his cologne as I slid in. Had he been smelling this good before?

I sat down in the car and placed my bags at my feet, reaching for the seat belt as I shifted to get comfortable. After I clicked my seat belt into place, I realized that Luke was still standing there holding the door. He had a faraway look in his eyes as he gazed at me, his eyes soft and his lips gently pressed together, staring at me as if he were noticing something for the first time.

"Um…" I started, giving him a wide-eyed expression. "You okay?"

"I'm good," he said and closed the door. I watched him with curiosity as he walked to the other side, his expression blank but his shoulders tense and square. What was his deal?

We rode in silence for a minute with the radio playing on low. A few times, I caught myself glancing at Luke out of the side of my eyes, but I could see that he was buried deep in his thoughts. I don't know what had happened with him between now and him asking if he could take me to work, but dude was acting all kinds of strange.

"You can stop here and I'll walk up," I told him about a block away from the entrance to my job.

"Here?" he frowned and then brought his eyes to my face for the first time since we'd got in the car. I nodded my head.

"Yeah… I don't think it's a good idea for you to drop me off right in front," I told him, hoping that I wouldn't have to explain any further.

"Oh." He nodded his head. He got it.

Grabbing my bag and my purse, I started to get out when I felt a light touch on my arm. Licking my lips, I ignored the flutters in my stomach and focused on him.

"I'm going to hit you up later on. Maybe we can hang out or some shit… That's cool?" he asked me and my heart skipped a beat.

"Yeah," I found myself saying. Then the devil on my shoulder decided this would be a good time to toy with his ass.

"But I thought I wasn't your type and now you're asking me for a date," I teased with a smile.

He gave me a blank stare and then his eyes twinkled as his smirk rose up on his face. He ran his tongue across his gold grill and it sent shivers through my whole body. I couldn't help but look at it… so thick, long and wide. There were probably so many things he could do with it. Things I hadn't had done to me in a long, long… long, long time.

"Who said anything about a date?" he inquired and I tilted my head to the side, questioning him with my eyes. "Unless you want it to be a date. You gon' be my baby mama after all."

"What?!" I quipped, jerking my head.

"Nothing."

He leaned in closer and I held my breath for a second, trying to adjust to the way that he was unknowingly setting my entire body on fire. Or maybe he did know just the effect that he had on me. I was sure it was the same as with all the women he met. He did happen to have a lot of lil' fans. I felt a pang of jealousy jolt through my chest when I thought of the girl he'd been playing with on the train.

"Um…" I cleared my throat but it did nothing to help me find the words to say.

"Do you want it to be a date?" he pressed on, his breath tickling the side of my face. It was cool... like Winterfresh cool. Mine, I'm sure, smelled just like coffee.

He pressed his finger into my leg and I snapped my head sideways to look at him, making my lips graze his on accident. A surge of electricity passed through me and it was like that simple touch awakened something in my soul. There was a magnetic pull between us and I knew I couldn't be the only one who felt it. Like I had a charge in my body that was drawing me to the warmth in his; seeking heat like a missile. I was erupting with lust and wanting what I never knew I had.

"Yes," I muttered before I could stop myself.

The air between us had become suffocating. The feelings swarming within me were much too powerful. I needed to get out before I did something stupid.

He snickered and I felt the throbbing between my thighs intensify to an all-time high. Leaning back, I glanced at him as he ran a solitary finger over the top of his lip, his eyes narrowed at me like he could see everything going on in my brain that I didn't want him to know.

"Then, it's a date. I'll hit you up," he said and then turned away, releasing me from his spell.

My body was finally capable of movement. I clutched my bags and purse in my hand and jumped out, scurrying away as fast as I could. As soon as I was only a few paces away, I heard the engine roar to life on Luke's Camaro as he pulled away.

A sad feeling washed over me before settling in my chest, when I turned around and saw that he had bent a corner and was out of sight. I felt like I'd left a piece of me when I got out of his car. A piece that was now with him and was there to stay.

Come Here, Rude Boy.

Carmella

There was nothing better than New York City, even at the start of, what seemed to be, a harsh winter. I loved every damn thing about this place.

Allow me to introduce myself. My name is Carmella Pickney, daughter of George and Luellen Pickney. But to my many fans on my Instagram page, I was @SexyCaramel69. Yes, I was smart, just like all of my sisters, but I had a hot body too and I loved the attention and privilege that came with it. There wasn't much that I wanted that didn't come easily to me because of my looks. If I wanted something, it didn't matter if it was from a man or a woman, they'd be falling over themselves to make it happen. Which was the exact reason I was utterly confused about the fact that it was so damn hard for me to catch a cab.

"SHIT!" I cursed as I watched yet another cab swerve by me and stop at another woman a few paces down from where I stood. Without even hesitating or acknowledging the fact that I'd been standing there much longer than her ass, the woman jumped right in the cab and it drove away.

"Bitch," I muttered and raised my hand up again.

A guy walked up with Beats headphones over his ears, bopping his head to the beat as he stood on the curb. I glanced at him, cutting my eyes when I saw him raise up two fingers to hail an approaching cab. Helllll naw! Not on my watch! The next cab that stopped, I was hopping my ass right in it, whether it had stopped for me or not.

Poking out my lips, I looked down the street and focused on the cab that was driving up. I stepped forward, closer to the edge, with my hand raised in the air. The guy kept bopping his head to the music in his ears.

I found myself looking at him, noticing that he was dressed in a nice ass style, but not really like what I was used to seeing in Cali or even in New York City. He had that ATL swag that I was accustomed to seeing back home. Brown skin, nice ass fade, a thin line of hair on his top lip and a little bit of a stubble on his bottom. Hmm, not bad.

The few seconds I had my eyes on him distracted me from the approaching cab, and my mouth dropped when I saw it swerve to a stop right in front of him.

"Oh *hell* naw!" I said as I watched him about to walk towards it and get inside.

How in the world did a Black man in New York City manage to get a cab before me? What was the world coming to?

Sucking my teeth, I walked forward quickly, jumping right in front of him, heading to the taxi.

"I'm sorry, but I've been standing here much longer than you," I told him without looking directly in his face. "This cab is mine."

"What?" he grumbled and I looked in his face, catching his frown. And his sexy ass eyes. Damn.

"Don't act like you didn't see me standing there when you walked up!" I snapped, ready to go off. Did I mention I had a bad ass attitude? Oh… well, I do.

"I ain't see shit," he replied with a frown on his face. He tried to push by me to the cab and I whipped around quickly, eager to get to it before he did.

Our hands reached for the door handle at the exact same time, but I knocked my duffle bag towards him, nudging him out of the way.

"Da *fuck*?!" he yelled just as I opened the door and tossed my things inside.

"What happened to ladies first?" I muttered to the cab driver who didn't seem the least bit interested in anything I had to say.

"This some fuckin' bullshit," the guy said just as I jumped inside.

Oh well. He could tell it to everybody else standing around and waiting for a taxi like his ass because I wasn't getting out. I went to close the door but he grabbed the handle, stopping me before I could.

"Move!" I yelled, yanking it hard. Frowning at the guy, I gritted my teeth and yanked even harder, ready to fight it out. I was not backing down.

"Hell naw!" he shot back, pulling it so hard that it ripped out of my grip. His ass almost made me break a damn nail!

"Scoot over!" he grumbled and I frowned up at him, ready to tell his ass off for yelling at me like that. He didn't know me! I might look pretty and all but I would whoop his ass!

"Who the hell you think you talking—"

"I said fuckin' *move*! I got somewhere to go so either scoot over or I'mma toss your lil' ass out."

His voice was low in volume but his tone had just the right amount of severity mixed with a malicious undertone that told me he wasn't playing around. That, matched with the fiery blaze in his eyes, made me close my mouth and scoot my ass over. My pride wouldn't let me give up the cab altogether but I no longer had a problem with sharing it.

"Where to?" the driver asked and I opened my mouth to tell him Janelle's address. But before I could even get it out, Rude Ass next to me gave out his.

"Headed to Brooklyn, boss," he informed the driver before rattling off the address like I wasn't sitting there glaring at him.

Crossing my arms, I didn't even try to hide the fact that I was mad as hell as I stared out the window beside me. He was lucky that I was heading to Brooklyn too.

We drove in silence as I looked outside of the window, being reminded of all the things I loved about this city. Originally, I had wanted to go to school in New York but Stanford was the school that offered me the scholarships. Still, I was set on going to NYU until Janelle convinced me otherwise. Looking back, I made the right choice. I loved the sun and the beach.

"Here you are," the cab driver said once we were in Brooklyn. "Where to for you?"

As Rude Ass pulled out his money to pay the driver, I gave him Janelle's address.

"Oh… well, you're here," the driver informed me once I'd finished.

"I'm here?" I looked around. What the hell was Janelle thinking? She lived in the damn hood!

"No, this can't be it. My sister wouldn't—"

"Yeah, the address you just told me is right there… the group of apartments on the corner. You want me to drive you to the corner?" he asked and I shook my head. "Okay, well, he just paid for your ride but I take tips."

Rolling my eyes, I grabbed my purse and searched for my wallet. I was annoyed by the driver mentioning that the asshole next to me had done anything for me.

"You could say 'thank you'. Damn," Rude Ass remarked as I pulled out some cash and gave it to the driver.

"Oh, now you want to be concerned with manners?" I huffed and watched him as he got out before sliding over to get out behind him. But I jumped when the door slammed closed, almost hitting me right in the face.

"That was so fuckin' rude!" I yelled just as I pushed the door open and stepped out, struggling to keep my balance while placing both of my bags on my shoulder.

"What?" he asked, frowning while pulling his headphones partially off his ear.

"You slammed the door in my face!"

"There are two doors. How the hell was I supposed to know you was gonna slide your ass over to get out of mine?" he replied, his frown deepening on his face.

He had a point but I still didn't like it.

"Niggas in this city ain't got no fuckin' manners!" I grumbled under my breath.

Taking off down the sidewalk, I ambled on with difficulty, my heavy duffle bag of clothes knocking me off balance with each step. Behind me, I heard his hefty footsteps and I rolled my eyes, noting that he was right behind me watching me struggle.

"I would ask you if you need a hand with that but niggas in this city ain't got no manners," I heard him say finally, a hint of sarcasm in his voice.

"I don't need no help," I replied back, snapping my neck with much attitude. Then, to my utter dismay, a big gust of wind decided to catch me in my lie, nearly knocking me fully off balance.

"Give me that."

I felt one hand on my side, steadying me onto my feet, as the other one plucked the duffle bag right from my shoulder.

"Wait, I can—"

But he pushed the headphones back on his ears, ignoring me as he walked a little bit ahead. The smoldering fire in me dimmed to a cool flame as I watched him, holding my bags while still bopping to his music. I couldn't help being grateful about him stepping in to help me carry my bag. Plus, he'd paid for my cab ride whether he'd meant to or not.

And he is sexy. The thought popped into my head so suddenly and I took another look at him, this time scrutinizing him from the back.

His pants were sagging a bit from his waist, showing off the top of his boxers whenever his white tee rose up a bit as he walked. The muscles in his arm flexed while he held onto my bag, making me lick my lips. He was definitely something nice to look at. His hair was cut low but he had enough waves to make a bitch seasick.

"This your stop?" he asked, turning around just as I was examining his ass. Tight and firm... just how I preferred it.

"Huh?"

He shuffled his feet, an annoyed expression ran through his eyes.

"Your. Stop. This it?"

"Uh," I checked the address on the door. "Yeah, this is it. Thank you for going out of you way to help me," I muttered as he handed me my bag. His arm muscles flexed again as he reached over, and my heart thumped loudly one good time. Daaaamn!

"It's not out the way or I wouldn't have done it. My grandmother stays a few blocks over and I'm headed to that spot on the corner over there," he told me, pointing his head towards the store he was referencing.

"Oh... well, I'm Carmella," I blurted out, feeling the need to lengthen the conversation. "I'm from Cali. Visiting my sister here."

He paused and looked at me with an intense expression, an unsaid thought running through his mind. Finally, he pressed his lips together and replied.

"I'm Cree."

Cree. Hmm… different but I liked it.

"Bye," he muttered before turning around and walking away. I watched him for a while, wondering if I would see him again. And then I wondered if I wanted to. Did I *really* want to see Cree again?

By the time I walked up the few steps to Janelle's door, the answer was already ringing loud in my mind as if someone was yelling it in my ears.

Yes. I definitely, *definitely* wanted to see Cree again.

Everything I Thought I Didn't Want

Janelle

"Hey, Janelle."

I turned around and watched as Chris jogged up to me. Stopping, he smiled as he fell into step right besides me. It was the end of another day, I was tired, and more than ready to go home. After starting my day with Luke, I was emotionally spent and now I was physically and mentally worn out from hours of work.

"Hey, how are you?" I asked, giving him a smile.

"Good. I wanted to ask you something," he started and I looked at him briefly before turning back around. I felt myself began to get anxious but also excited as I wondered what it was that he needed to ask me.

"What is it?"

"Well," he began and then reached out to grab my arm, stopping me from walking. Then he turned around so that he was standing right in my face. My nervous jitters grew nearly into a full on spasm.

"I've been trying to hang out with you for a while… alone," he began and my breathing slowed. "I would love to be able to take you out sometime."

Oh God!

"On a date," he clarified.

"Really?" I asked, not even bothering to think about how desperate I may have sounded. I sincerely couldn't believe what he was saying. Chris Havarty was asking me on a date. In less than twenty-four hours, two men had asked me on a date. Me. The nerdy, introverted lawyer chick who was barely ever asked anywhere.

"Yeah, I've been trying to for a minute but… things kept getting in the way," he told me, emphasizing the word 'things'.

"Yeah, I know. I thought you had a thing for Tatiana," I admitted with a smile. And then my smile dropped instantly as I wondered if I'd gone too far.

"I mean—"

"No, I can see why you thought that. But I've just been being nice to her because I think she likes me."

Of *course* she likes you, I wanted to say. Men were so dumb sometimes.

"But I'm not into her like that. I prefer women who look like the ones in my family, if you know what I mean."

I smiled brightly. I knew exactly what he meant.

"Okay… well, yes. I would love to go out with you," I told him and he nodded his head, seeming satisfied with my answer.

"Great. I'll give you a call," he replied.

He turned around and took off in the other direction, leaving me swirling in my feelings, running each word through my mind, unbelieving that it had actually happened. Chris asked me out on a date.

Turning around, I started back walking and my eyes fell on a red car just as it passed by me. I felt a thump in my chest as I bent my neck to see who it was, a glitter of hope passing through my body. But it wasn't a red Camaro.

Wow… Two seconds after being all excited about Chris, the thought of him was totally washed away the second that I thought I saw Luke. What was wrong with me?

Something is seriously wrong.

I ran my hand over my face, thinking about the fact that I'd just accepted dates from two different men. One who was everything I *thought* I wanted and the other… everything I thought I didn't.

***

By the time Carmella came in my room barking about how I needed to hurry my ass up and get dressed, I wasn't ready to go any damn where. She'd only been at my spot for a few hours and already she knew my neighbors better than me. When I got home, she happily informed me that the chick next door had told her that we needed to stop at some party at some club around the corner because it would be 'poppin'. Apparently, this club was the neighborhood spot and the place to be every Friday and Saturday night. Didn't seem like my type of scene at all, but Carmella was sold and I'd promised her I'd go out so I was shit out of luck.

"Jani, are you ready yet? Damn! You barely wear makeup so what the hell is taking you so long?!" Carmella yelled, bursting right into my room. I slipped my feet into some heels and rolled my eyes at her.

"I'm coming!" Grabbing my clutch, I walked out of the room and then stopped, wondering if I needed to grab some flats in case my feet started hurting.

"What's wrong *now*?" Carmella asked, rolling her eyes at me before following it up with a groan. She was such a brat. It wasn't like she was a stranger to going out and shaking her ass but now she wanted to give me a hard time.

"Five seconds. I just need to grab some flats in case—"

"Hell naw!" Carmella griped, grabbing me by my arm as she began to tug me forward. "Skip the granny shoes for one night, bitch. We are about to have fun. Here, take this."

I looked at what was in her hand and knew that it was the devil in a glass. See, let me explain. Carmella always managed to bring out the bad side in me. Remember when I said I used to sneak out the house when I was in high school so I could party on the southside of Atlanta? That was all Carmella's doing and she was at it again.

"What is in here?" I asked, squinting at the shot glass in my hand before scrutinizing the dark liquid. She grinned in my face and I swear I saw her eyes flash red like a demon. Whatever she had up in that glass was about to get me fully fucked up.

"Just some new shit they're doing in Cali. Try it."

Peer pressure was a bitch. But deep down, I couldn't say I didn't want to go out and have a good time. And I knew as soon as I heard that Carmella was in the city, that the turn up was going to begin. So why not?

PORSCHA STERLING

Tossing my head back, I drained the shot in one gulp and winced when I felt it burn all the way down. Shit. It was so damn *disgusting*.

"Follow it up with this," Carmella urged, pushing something else in my hand as I tried to swallow down the taste on my tongue. "It'll kill the burn."

I tossed back the next glass, realizing a little too late that what she'd given me to 'kill the burn' was more alcohol. But it was lemon flavored and tasted good as hell.

"Ready?" she asked, a hint of a smile on the edge of her lips.

"Yeah," I replied back with a goofy grin of my own. I was already beginning to feel at ease.

"Val? You're coming?" I asked and knocked on her door.

"No!" she yelled out. "I'm studying. I'll go next time."

Eyes growing wide, I shrugged and linked arms with Carmella. I was ready to go.

Since the party was only about a block away, we decided to walk. With each step, the drunker I became. But I handled my liquor well so no one could really tell.

"There it is," Carmella said, pointing ahead to a big building that didn't look like much of anything on the outside.

However, you could hear the music loud as hell so it was obvious there was a party going on inside. There was a line of people standing outside the door, all trying to get in and I groaned.

"Look at that line," I complained, sucking my teeth.

"Don't worry about that. Sidney told me to call her when we got here and she'd get us in," Carmella said, pecking on the screen of her phone.

"Sidney?"

"Your neighbor," she replied with a roll of her eyes. "Damn, do you talk to her at all? She lives right next door."

Um… no. I didn't talk to anyone around here because I stayed my ass at home unless I was going to work.

"You made it!" Sidney said as she walked out.

Sidney walked out looking slightly more dressed up than normal. She was a tomboy and I rarely saw her in more than some sweatpants and a hoody or shirt with some Jordans to match. I'd always assumed she was a lesbian. Tonight, she was wearing some nice black jeans that showed she had something of a shape, but I couldn't really tell since they were a little baggy. She paired it with a button-up shirt and some nice black boots. Her long hair was still pulled up into a tight ponytail.

Smiling at Sidney, I followed behind her and Carmella as she led us past the line and into the club.

No More Fuckin' Wit' Lames.

Janelle

I looked at the crowd as Carmella laughed with Sidney like they were old friends, and immediately was grateful that I'd allowed her to dress me. Chicks in New York knew how to dress. Not like they didn't where I was from but the style wasn't what I was used to.

It was pretty cold outside so almost everyone, including me, had on some variation of high heeled boots. Being that it was cold, I wanted to match my boots up with a pair of black pants and a purple turtleneck, but Carmella cursed me out so bad that I caught an attitude and told her to dress me.

When she showed me the flaming red bodycon dress that she wanted me to wear, it was *my* time to curse *her* out. It was November in Brooklyn and cold as hell. Who would be wearing that shit? But she won the war so I put it on and just grabbed a coat to wear until I got inside. Turns out, she'd picked just the right outfit.

"Damn… Christmas came early, nigga! Look at they fine asses!" a man exclaimed as we walked inside.

I looked over at him, curious about what he looked like. As soon as I saw him, I wished I hadn't. He stuck his tongue out at me, showing off a bright red stain in the middle from whatever he had been sipping on. Not sexy. His friend was cute though. I ducked my head and smiled at him when our eyes met. I was already feeling the liquor. Shit. This was going to be a crazy night.

"I hope it's better lookin' niggas inside of here than what we saw coming in," Carmella said to Sidney, and I nodded my head in agreement as I fell into step beside them.

"Oh it will be," Sidney told her. "The Murray brothers will be here and they always draw a crowd of fine ass goons out because they cool wit' every damn body."

"The *who* brothers?" I chimed in, feeling a stirring feeling in the pit of my stomach.

"The Murrays… you know 'em? They all fine as hell. My girl 'bout to have a baby by one of the older ones, wit' her lucky ass. The only thing 'bout them is they run up in *everything*… especially the one named Outlaw. His ass be stacking bitches left and right," she continued, filling us both in, and I noted that she definitely liked men.

I felt a burning sensation in my chest when she mentioned Luke being with other women. But he wasn't mine so I shook it off. I had no reason to be jealous. It wasn't like he was my man.

"They sound hot," Carmella said, her eyes scanning the club. "I met this cute guy earlier. Hopefully, I'll see him here."

Just then the DJ dropped the beat on a song that had everybody in the club jumping to their feet and singing along. Including me. Yes… I know it's a bit of a surprise that I would know any rap song at all. But I was one of those smart, nerdy chicks who listened to trap music all day long. There wasn't a song by 2 Chainz or Young Thug that I didn't know.

"C'mon! Let's dance!" Carmella yelled and snatched me into the middle of the floor before I could even say no.

One thing for sure, I had rhythm and I could get down when the beat hit me just right. Although dancing was usually something that I kept to myself in the privacy of my own room, when Carmella and I got together, she turned me into a new person. Three songs in and we were still dancing, twerking and winding our bodies on the floor, fitting right in with the crowd.

"Oh shit!" the DJ yelled all of a sudden, turning down the music. "There go my muthafuckin' niggas! Everybody give it up for Kane, Tank, Dent, Yolo and Outlaaaaawwww!"

My heart stopped in my chest as everyone yelled and screamed with their hands in the air. Turning towards where they all were staring, I looked just in time to see Luke and his brothers walking into the club. Women all around me shrieked and yelled their names, trying to get their attention as they came through looking like hood royalty.

Luke was dressed simply in some designer black sweatpants with black, gold and white shoes, a black hoodie underneath a black and gold t-shirt, and his neck adorned with multiple gold chains. He had his hair braided but it was loose at the ends and pulled up in a messy bun, showing off the bling in each of his ears, and the diamond watch on his wrist glistened under the dim lighting as he moved. In his hand was a plastic cup that he sipped out of as he staggered in, walking like he had a damn baseball bat between his legs.

"I need a drink," I told Carmella before running off to the bar.

Her eyes were stuck on the main attraction of the moment, the Murray brothers. She probably had no idea that I'd even left.

"What you havin'?" the bartender, a young guy with fresh dreads asked as he glanced in my direction.

"A shot of the strongest whatever you got," I blurted out. "Make that two of them." He smiled, showing off a row of white teeth. He was cute.

"A'ight, I got somethin' special I'll mix up for you," he said, running his tongue along the inside of his mouth.

Letting out a breath, I nodded and twisted around, trying to appear as normal as possible. Glancing over to where Luke was, I instantly became annoyed when I saw him smiling and whispering in the ear of a girl that was sitting on his lap. As the music played, she danced on him, grinding her ass into him as he ran his hands up and down her body, kissing her on her neck while she giggled.

"Here," the bartender said, pulling my attention away from Luke's thot-show. Thank God. Watching was making me sick to my stomach.

I grabbed the first shot glass and frowned at the murky pink liquid inside before shooting a look at the bartender who was smiling at me with his arms crossed, anxiously waiting for me to take it.

"Let me know what you think," he instructed, just as I swallowed the first one down with my eyes squeezed shut.

I was expecting it to taste nasty and burn going down but it was good as hell. Whatever he made tasted like Juicy Juice. Reaching back on the counter, I grabbed the other glass and gulped that down as well.

"That was good," I told him, licking the remainder of the liquid from my lips.

"You won't need anything else the rest of the night. Bet," he winked and shot me a smile before walking away.

"I'll be the judge of that," I told him, giving him a flirty smile of my own before leaving.

Fifteen minutes later, all I could say was that the bartender hadn't told a lie. The drink he made had me feeling good as hell.

"Oh this is my sooooong!" I said, throwing my hands in the air just as "Do It" by Mykko Montana came on.

"Uh huh," Carmella replied and I frowned, looking at her. She seemed out of it, biting the inside of her cheek as she concentrated on something.

"What's with you?" I asked her, turning around so I could see what she was looking at.

"I saw a guy this morning when I was on my way to your spot. He was an asshole... tried to steal my cab. He's here," she said, gesturing over near where Luke was sitting and my lips parted slightly as I looked over. "The one with the black New York fitted cap."

Although she was motioning to the guy next to him, my attention fell on Luke, who was still being entertained by the same woman while two others stood around him, flirting and smiling as if they were waiting their turn. Ripping my attention away from him, I focused instead on the one that Carmella was referring to. He was sitting right next to Luke, smoking a blunt and sipping from his cup as if he was in his own world.

"Well, if he's such an asshole, why you worried about him?" I asked her with a frown. "I've been wanting to dance but all you've been doing is sitting here like you trying to look cute!"

I started winding in my seat to the song as I looked at her. The beat was about to drop and I was ready to drop my ass right with it. It was terrible the things that liquor did to me. That's why I stuck to wine and tried to avoid anything dark. Dark liquor pulled out the ratchet bitch in me that I didn't know I had, and tequila pulled out the undercover hoe in me that I tried to ignore.

"I'm wondering if I should go over there and say something to him," she explained, catching me off guard.

In all the time I'd known Carmella, which was since the day she was born, never had she seemed nervous about speaking to anyone. In fact, of all of my sisters, Carmella and Vonia had always been the most outgoing.

"Well, while you're sitting here trying to figure that out, I'm going to dance," I told her, eyeing a semi-cute guy on the dancefloor who was staring at me. He wasn't all that but he'd do for now. I just wanted to have a good time since I'd been dragged out of the house.

We can start off on dis floor

End up on that bed

You rubbin' through my head

While I'm all between yo' legs

I'mma hit it from the front, back, side, side

Giiiirl, I love the way you

Do it...

I was in my own world, in the middle of the crowd, dancing like I'd lost my mind. The song changed and I felt hands on me. A small voice in my mind was telling me to snap on whoever it was grabbing me from behind, but the alcohol in me was saying grind up on that nigga. So I did.

"You tryin' to have fun tonight?" the man behind me asked, pushing his lips up against my ear. I cut my eyes at him, smiling when I saw it was the guy I saw earlier on the dancefloor who I thought was cute.

"That's why I'm here," I replied, shrugging. The music slowed down and we went into a slow grind. It had been a long time since I'd had sex and I could feel the stirring in between my thighs begging me to answer its request for dick.

In the middle of dancing up on the guy behind me, I looked up and found myself staring right into Luke's eyes. I almost froze in place. He had a straight, emotionless look almost like he was forcing himself to keep a straight face. But his eyes told everything. They were focused on me and I could almost see the flame in them as he stared hard, eyes ablaze for some reason I didn't understand.

I kept my attention on him as I danced, feeling like I was putting on a show for him, for some reason. The alcohol was making me do things that I'd never had the nerve to do otherwise, but I was feeling good as hell. Licking my lips, I shot him a look, running my eyes up and down over him sending him strong fuck signals as I grinded on the man behind me. But he continued to give me the stone-faced expression. Leaning forward, he whispered something in the ear of the girl on his lap, and I saw her face fall before she got up.

Luke stood up and I kept my eyes on him as he began walking, his eyes concentrated on me. My breath caught my lungs and I felt myself began to get excited. As he came into the crowd, chicks began to turn towards him and reach out, grabbing on any part of him they could touch but he pressed forward, only pausing to politely pull women from off of him.

"Aye, you wanna get up out of here?" the guy behind me asked and I felt him kiss me on my neck.

"Huh?" I asked, remembering that he was behind me. I was still dancing but I was so focused on Luke that I'd totally forgotten he was behind me.

"You wanna leave?" he repeated just as Luke walked up on us.

I was confused by the look in his eyes. He seemed angry as hell and it caught me all the way off guard, stealing the words from my lips. No longer looking at me, he focused on the guy behind me and I felt the guy's body tense up right before he backed up.

"Nigga, what da *fuck* you doin' here?" Luke began, pulling his hand close to his side. My eyes cut down to it, wondering if he was holding a gun.

"Da fuck you mean, Law? I ain't allowed here no more?"

Stepping back, I backed away, not wanting to be caught in between whatever it was that the two of them had going on. Others on the dancefloor backed away as well as the music got lower. People began whispering around me, everyone trying to figure out what the hell was going on.

"Hell naw, you ain't allowed here no more, fuck nigga!" Luke sneered through his teeth as he pulled out his gun from his side. "Coward ass muthafucka!"

Eyes-wide, I wondered if I was about to witness my first homicide. I wanted to run away but I was stuck, frozen in place. I'd never seen a gun before. It was almost like I didn't know how the hell to react. This was the kind of shit I watched on TV, not something I'd ever expected to be part of.

Suddenly, there was movement from the side of the club and I watched as Luke's brothers all stood up and filed over, ready to back him up, if necessary. They stood a little behind where he was, giving him his own space but ready when the time came.

"Nigga, we beefin'?" the guy asked, his eyes narrowed as he looked at Luke. "I ain't got no issues wit' you, bruh."

"I got a fuckin' issue wit' you, punk ass nigga. How da fuck you let yo' fuckin' sister get raped by dat fuck nigga and get lost when it's time to handle that shit?! I almost caught a fuckin' case over some shit *you* shoulda fuckin' handled, ole pussy ass bitch." Luke's words were like venom as he spewed them, each one making me flinch even though they weren't directed at me. "Get out my fuckin' sight. I don't fuck wit' lames and I don't fuck wit' pussy niggas."

Turning, I looked from Luke to the guy he was speaking to and watched as they glared at each other, each malicious stare delivering unspoken words that the other understood. Finally, the guy shrugged and shook his head, muttering words under his breath as he turned to leave. Luke stood there and watched him until he got out of the club.

"Damn! Well, if you didn't know it, the muthafuckin' Outlaw is up in dis bitch!" the DJ said, hollering over the loudspeaker. "Now that he done regulated this shit, let's get back to the fuckin' party!"

And with that, a Drake song came up on the speakers and people started partying as if what had just occurred was commonplace in the hood. Maybe it was. Luke turned to me, his eyes still on fire and I looked away, wondering if it was my turn, for him to turn his anger on me for unknowingly dancing with his enemy.

"What you doin' out here?" he asked, making me look up. His eyes weren't on my face at all. Instead, he was eyeing my attire and I felt shy all of a sudden, wondering if he liked what he saw.

"My sister said she heard from my neighbor that this was the place to be," I told him, finally able to find my voice.

"Naw, this ain't the place to be," he said, his eyes still raking my body and I blushed when he licked his lips. "Come with me."

Not waiting for me to respond, he laced his fingers in mine and started to pull me away.

"But my sister—" I started but stopped short when I saw that Carmella had finally decided to approach the guy she'd been pointing at. They were having what seemed like a deep conversation and she was not the least bit worried about me.

Luke pulled me over to where he had been sitting with his brothers, and I felt my stomach flip-flop when I saw how many other women were looking at me with jealous looks in their eyes. I immediately picked up on the way they each sized me up, making their own judgments as to whether or not I deserved the attention of the infamous Outlaw.

"Who knew you could work your hips like that?" Luke whispered in my ear as he placed his body behind mine. His hands traveled down to my hips and I closed my eyes, overwhelmed by the feeling that took over me.

The DJ must have been getting cues from Luke on what to do because it was like he knew that we needed something to grind to. The song stopped and he began to play "Grind on Me" by Pretty Ricky, a song that never got old when you was in the club with somebody sexy as hell right after having something good to drink.

"Dance with me, baby," Luke instructed, his hands running all over my body. The sound of his voice put me in a hypnotic state and it was like I wasn't aware of anyone else other than him. His body was pressed against mine and he dropped his face into my neck, running his lips right against my hot spot. My body was tingling and my emotions were high.

Part of why I didn't like to drink was because I was a controlled person. In my sober state, I could ignore how I really wanted to react to things and reason myself into acting how I *should* instead. But with a little bit of drink in me, I operated all on what I wanted to do and gave no fucks as to what everyone else expected of me. And in this instance? I wanted to fuck Luke. I wanted to let go and allow him to do to me everything that he wanted to do. I would probably regret it later but I wasn't worried about that right now.

Opening his mouth, Luke ran his tongue along my neck and over my shoulder, making me bite my lip as I gushed with honey, totally soaking my panties.

"Don't let me catch you fuckin' wit' lames no more," he told me and I slowly nodded my head. I would have agreed to any damn thing right then and I knew that he understood that when I heard him laugh a little at my response.

Turning me around, I finally opened my eyes and the lust in me grew to another level, totally overpowering me and crushing every inhibition that I formerly had. I wanted him.

"Can I take you home?" he asked before further clarifying. "Now?"

"Yes," I said, nodding my head. He bent down and kissed me on my lips, lightly at first before deepening the embrace, pulling my bottom lip into his and then parting my lips so he could suck on my tongue.

Damn... he could kiss good as hell. And, no, he didn't taste like old sock drawer pennies. Matter of fact, I could have probably had an orgasm just off his kiss. He was just that good. Before I knew it, I was grinding up against him and he had pushed his hand between us, rubbing at my hard nipples through my dress.

"Fuck..." he whispered against my lips, pulling away. "I want you." There was a rugged need in his voice when he said it and I creamed on the spot.

God... he was so sexy.

"Let's go," he said, finessing his facial hair before grabbing my hand and looking around the club. I glanced over at Carmella and saw that she was posted up on the wall still talking to the same guy. She had a crazy look on her face but was fully involved in whatever they were talking about.

"That your sister?" Luke asked, following my stare and I nodded my head. "That's my brother. He'll make sure she gets home."

I hesitated for a moment, looking from Luke back to Carmella and then nodded my head. Still on an emotional high, I allowed him to lead me out the club. I felt like the luckiest girl on Earth.

The Ultimate Bad Boy.

Janelle

*L*uke and I didn't say a single word to each other as he drove me back to my place. Each of us knew what was about to happen and we were ready for it. I was probably more ready than he was, to be honest.

It had been so long since I'd had sex with someone that I couldn't even remember when the last time was or who it was with. Yeah, it sounds like I'm a hoe, doesn't it? Well, let me clear something up for you: every woman has a little bit of undercover hoe in them. There are plenty of times where we look at a man and wonder how it would be to fuck him. Doesn't mean we want to play house with him and make him our man. We just want to fuck. Nothing wrong with that.

"This you, right?" Luke asked, pulling off to the side of the road right in front of my apartment.

"Yes," I told him and then I suddenly remembered that Val was inside. How the hell did I forget Val?

"Let me check inside to make sure it's good for you to come in," I told him and he gave me a confused look before it finally clicked what I was saying.

"Right," he muttered, nodding his head. "I'll be here."

He licked his lips and ran his eyes over my body one more time, and it put some fire under my ass to hurry up so I could get him inside. Unlocking the door, I walked into the dark house, not turning on any lights as I crept over to Val's room. Her door was open and I could hear her snoring softly, so I eased the door closed and tiptoed back outside. Once I signaled to Luke that he could come in, he shut off his car and got up. I watched him walk to the door with my heart thumping my chest as I admired his sexy style.

He had his hands stuffed in his pockets as he strode coolly and confidently to the door, with his legs wide like he was holding a monster in his pants. I couldn't wait to find out.

"Shhh," I instructed with a finger to my lips as he came in. I closed the door behind him and grabbed his hand, leading him to my room.

His hands were on me before we could make it there, pulling my body against his as he started kissing me on my neck. He pulled my dress up my thighs, and slipped his hands down through the front of my panties just as we got to my door and I froze, closing my eyes and biting my bottom lip as he began running his fingers over my clit like an expert. We hadn't even made it into the room and I was about to come up on my first orgasm.

"You like that?" he whispered but instead of answering with my mouth, my legs began to tremble, letting him know that he was doing everything just right.

He removed his fingers from me and turned me around to face him then dipped down, kissing me as he lifted me up like I weighed nothing more than a few pounds. Kicking off my heels, I wrapped my arms around his neck and my legs around his waist, feeling him fiddling with something beneath my ass.

He broke our kiss for a few seconds and I saw him place a condom wrapper in his mouth, tearing off the top. I looked up at him, somewhat shocked that he had even thought to use one without me mentioning it. I felt him placing the rubber on his dick as he cradled me in his arms, walking forward a little so he could nudge the door closed.

Neither one of us wanted to wait to get fully undressed, we wanted it just that bad. Leaning against the door, Luke lifted me up, holding my hips between his hands, and then lowered me slowly, right on the top of his dick.

Let me pause right here.

I was far from a virgin and far from an amateur. In fact, I actually considered myself to be pretty experienced on my shit when it came to sex. I loved it to the point that I studied it. My need to know it all didn't just apply to when I was in law school. It applied to everything I liked. If I enjoyed something, I would research it, wanting to learn as much about it.

So when it came to sex, I did the same thing and I tried all kinds of things: Yoni eggs, various toys and lubricants, Ben Wa balls... everything. The one thing I hadn't tried was anal, but that was only because I hadn't been with anyone I really wanted to do it with. That said, just trust that I knew what I was doing. But with Luke... it was much different.

After he eased me onto his lap and slid up inside of my walls, I instantly understood exactly what all the fuss was when it came to him. He hadn't even started stroking me yet and I was about to lose my mind. His dick was big, thick, hard as hell, but the one thing that had me about to go absolutely insane was the fact that his dick had a curve to it. A crazy curve, almost like a hook, and that shit was tapping right on my damn G-spot.

I was soaking wet so I slid onto him, taking all of him in without much resistance. When he was all the way in, he leaned back against the wall, not moving and not saying anything for a second, both of us enjoying the way we felt to each other.

"Damn..." he moaned.

He started working his hips and my head fell back. My mouth was open as I held onto him, not wanting to wind my hips or anything for fear that I would cum in five seconds flat. He felt just that good inside of me. Grabbing my hips, he started moving them for me, as he slid himself in and out slowly in a rhythmic motion that set my soul on fire, and made every nerve in me shoot off like mini explosions in my body.

"Fuck this shit," I heard him say all of a sudden and he lifted me up, pulling completely out of me. My eyes snatched open in surprise and disappointment, immediately missing the feel of him inside.

Leaning over, he laid me down on the bed and started taking his clothes off.

"Take all that shit off," he instructed me. "I wanna see everything."

Smirking, I eased out my dress as he took off his clothes and then leaned over to turn on the small radio beside my bed, connecting it to my iPod to let one of my playlists play. Then I cut on the dim reading light beside my bed, partially illuminating the room.

"You sexy, yo," he mumbled as he looked at me while standing up, as he ran his hand over his erect dick.

I let my eyes fall over his body, examining every bit of it, including the tattoos that fully covered him before focusing in on the pole in his hand. He was sexy too, in a way that I'd never expected I'd be attracted to. The ultimate bad boy, everything that I was raised not to want but, in this moment, he was exactly what I needed.

Luke leaned down and guided me down onto my back by pressing on my shoulder. I sucked in a breath of anticipation, excited about being able to feel him again but a little nervous at the same time. Something about Luke made me feel like he was about to lay some shit on me that had me walking away not knowing my name, and dickmatized out of this world.

Parting my thighs, Luke hovered over me, looking between my legs before dipping two fingers straight into my hole. I gasped and closed my eyes tight, enjoying the feeling of him stirring his fingers inside of me. He moved like an expert who knew exactly how to get his desired reaction. I wasn't the only one who studied this shit.

Placing a hand on each side of my waist, he pulled me down and began kissing up my flat stomach, sucking and licking in between until he came right up to my small breasts. He eyed them hungrily, hesitating only a second to lick his lips before opening his mouth and lowering it right over my nipple. He made figure eights around my nipple with his tongue, teasing me in a way that felt so good, before he finally began to suck gently on it, pulling hard and nearly sending my body into convulsions.

I didn't feel like I could take anymore but he felt like it was the perfect time to push me a bit further, sticking his two fingers back into me, stirring my honey.

"Fuck…" I moaned, arching my back and pressing my body more into him as I struggled to keep my orgasm at bay. But Luke wasn't having that shit.

"Cum for me," he ordered and that was all it took. His words spoke directly to my body, ordering it to do as he said, against the urgings of my mind. I came in seconds, shivering and moaning so loud as I clutched onto him, digging my nails hard into his back. His fingers were inside me the entire time, each movement erupting another spasm inside of me until I was sent into a state of utter confusion. I was telling him to stop, but wrapping my legs around him and pushing my hips against his hand all at the same damn time.

Lifting up, Luke sat up, pressing the palms of his hands flat on the bed on either side of my head as he stared into my eyes. I felt his legs nudge my legs apart and I sucked in a breath, knowing what was coming next. He entered me with ease, this time feeling even harder than before, and I gasped again, adjusting my hips to meet his width.

Sex with me is so amazing…

Rihanna's song became the perfect background music to our intimate dance as he began to stroke me like a pro, making me wince with pleasure each time that he tapped against my G-spot.

I came four times to his one but that was only the first round. After lying next to each other for only about five minutes, Luke reached over, pinched my nipple and I groaned, pushing my ass against him.

He was already hard so he slipped another condom on and we were at it again.

Sang That Beyoncé for a Nigga.

Carmella

"I want you to go deep, baby," I cooed, licking my lips in the dark. "I can't wait to feel that big dick."

Cree leaned back and I saw the faint outline of a smirk on his face as he peered at me in the dark. I shot him my most seductive stare, biting my bottom lip and throwing my soft eyes on him as I wiggled my hips in anticipation, waiting for him to put it on me.

Now, before you go assuming anything, let me just put this out there now. I am not a hoe. But I do have hoe tendencies. Make sense? I don't fuck just any ole nigga but I don't have any problem with jumping into bed with one if I felt like he could please me. And what was wrong with that? As long as he wrapped it up, who cares that I had no problem fuckin' a nigga I just met and going on 'bout my business?

Even so, Cree was a special case because, in all honesty, I shouldn't have been in the bed with his ass. He was a pure asshole in all ways, and nothing about him was anything like what I liked. Matter of fact, we spent most of the time in the club arguing and throwing jabs at each other. I couldn't stand his ass and he seemed like he couldn't stand me either but, for some reason, neither of us would walk away. We just stood there arguing the whole night, nitpicking at each other over some silly shit.

Every single thing I did, he had something to say about it and it pissed me off. In fact, when I walked over to speak to him after his brother went crazy on some nigga in the club, the first thing out his mouth was, 'You look like you thirst trappin' tonight'.

What kind of shit was that to say? I was in the club so that's how I was dressed and I looked damn good, might I add. Plenty of niggas had been trying to get my attention but I'd blown them off while trying to figure out a way to get at him.

"Thirst trappin'?" I asked him, frowning. "Is that your way of saying I look nice?"

He looked me dead in my eyes, not a trace of a smile or anything else on his face.

"No."

That was all I needed to catch an attitude. How dare he tell me that shit? I may have not been the finest bitch in the room, in his book, but I was definitely on point and I'd be damned if he tell me differently. To add to that, I had over 50K followers on Instagram to prove that my body was banging. And my shit was real too… I worked hard as hell on it to make sure it stayed that way. This ass didn't come easy!

"Why the fuck you so fuckin' rude?" I asked, placing my hand on my hip as I glared at him.

A hint of something passed through his eyes and he dropped his head, lowering his gaze to focus right on me.

"It ain't in me to be no other kinda way, ma," he said, a southern

140

accent shining through. "If you don't like it, get da fuck on. I didn't ask your ass to walk over here."

"You know what? Fuck you!" I shot back, feeling even more heated. "I came over here to speak and here you go with this bullshit."

He started to laugh and it caught me off-guard. No man had ever got me more pissed than he was doing in this moment.

"What, you mad because a nigga ain't actin' like what you used to? Playin' into your lil' trap with ease and fallin' all over himself tryin' to fuck just 'cause you want it?" he battled, his eyes narrowed into mine.

"What the hell makes you think I want shit from you?" I asked him. "You ain't cute! Matter of fact, you ain't shit! Actin' like I'mma kiss your ass over some dick. I don't know about all these *other* bitches in here but I don't want shit that you got and—"

Grabbing my hand, he stepped forward, pressing his body closer to mine and then pushed my hand up inside the front of his shirt, allowing it to graze over his rock hard abs. Got *damn*, he had it going on up underneath his clothes and how he knew that I was crazy over a nigga with muscles, I have no idea. I explored his body liberally, feeling all over his chest as he watched the expressions change on my face. Then, smirking, I glanced up at him and started to push my hands south, licking my lips as I rubbed over the V that led to the one muscle I really was curious about.

"Naw," he said, nudging my hand out of the way and taking a step back. "No free passes, ma."

Rolling my eyes, I put my hand on my hip and sucked my teeth. Looking at me, he sipped the drink in his cup before pushing it into my hands like he wanted me to throw it away for him.

"Um…"

"Drink some," he told me, his eyes lowering to my body even though he still had the furrow-browed, 'no bullshit' expression on his face. Watching him watch me, I went ahead and started sipping.

About an hour later, we tried to have a normal conversation and get to know each other but he'd always say something to fuck up the vibe. It was like he didn't know how to talk to a woman and was constantly pissing me off. Even so, when he told me he was going to drive me back to Janelle's place since she was gone, I knew I didn't want to spend the night alone and I couldn't help that I was attracted to him and a bit curious. I was only going to be in New York for a week so might as well have fun.

And that's how I ended up here.

"C'mon," I begged, ready to get started. "I'm ready for it."

"A'ight, but you need to stop that big dick shit," he told me as he slipped his boxers down while leaning over me. I squinted in the dark, trying to see what he was working with but I couldn't see a damn thing.

"I only got what da fuck I was born with. And it ain't much… but you gon' take these four inches and work with that shit."

"WHAT?!" I almost yelled, ready to jump out of the fuckin' bed. Four inches wasn't even worth me taking my clothes off for!

"Lay down," he said and pushed me down on my back. I was about to tell him to get the hell off but he silenced me with a kiss while parting my legs with his hand, steadying himself over my body.

Damn. He knew what he was doing with that kiss. He played games with my tongue, sucking on it and nibbling gently on the tip, making me relax. Shit… even if it was only four inches that he was working with, it was obvious that his tongue game was on point. Maybe I could at least get him to suck on the pussy a bit to make up for the small dick.

Then, before I even had a chance to react, Cree pushed forward, leaning his entire body into me as he eased himself into my velvet walls. My mouth fell open as I realized that his ass was a muthafuckin' lie. Wasn't nothing little about what the hell he was working with. He wasn't too big but he wasn't small either. In fact, he fit in my shit just right, filling me completely. But his width was another damn thing. He had a fat ass dick and I could feel him on all four walls.

"Gotdamn, gotdamn, gotdamn!" I cursed when he continued pushing in well past what I expected.

"That's right, baby," he cooed into my ear and I could feel his lips forming a smirk. "Sang that Beyoncé for a nigga."

This fool was crazy.

I started slow grinding my hips against him, but he stunned me when he grabbed the headboard behind my head and began to stroke into me at a fast pace, speeding up steadily as he rocked the shit out of my body. I couldn't even keep up with this shit but I gritted my teeth and matched his pace. But every time I did, he sped up even faster until eventually, I just lifted my hips and wrapped my legs around his waist, letting him have his way because it felt soooo good.

I learned quickly that Cree liked everything rough and he was aggressive as hell in the bed. After fucking me missionary style for a few minutes, he pulled one of my legs all the way back until it was over his shoulder and drilled into me hard as I dug my nails into his neck.

"Harder," he told me and I opened my eyes, wondering what he meant. "Dig harder."

His ass had a thing for pain but, if that's what he liked, I was ready to give it to him. And he gave it right back to my ass too, digging all up in my guts to the point that I didn't know if I could take it anymore. Gritting my teeth, I flexed my feet and curled my toes as I bore it. I wanted him to stop but I also wanted more.

Then he slowed down, stroking gently as he dropped his head, biting hard on my body. I winced but, for some reason it turned me on. Nobody had ever done this to me before. He matched the pain with pleasure as he continued biting on me while grinding his dick into my pleasure spot. I was in awe of him. He knew what I liked even better than I did because I couldn't have imagined this shit.

"Face down, ass up," he said, and I jumped to do exactly what he asked. Tooting my ass in the air, I turned around and slapped it, ready for him to get started.

He came up behind me, pulling my ass up even higher, deepening my arch before pushing in while winding my hair around his fist and pulling hard. He gripped my waist with the other hand, using it as leverage as he drilled forcefully into me.

"OH GOD!" I cried out, creaming instantly. I came so fast and hard that I started to see spots and felt like I was about to black out. As soon as I came down from my high, I started to feel weak but he wasn't done yet. Grabbing one leg, he held it up in the air as he continued to pound me from behind, pulling my hair so hard that I thought he was going to snatch it from my scalp. But still I didn't want him to stop.

"FUCK!" I yelled out when I felt the next orgasm approaching.

It was even more powerful than the first. This time he came with me, swirling his dick in circles before delivering short jabs right to my center, as he stroked the hell out of my kitty before collapsing next to me on the bed.

"Shit…" was all he said and I just lay there, totally paralyzed and unable to move, wondering what the fuck had just happened.

***

"CREE! Who the hell is this you got in my house?!" a voice yelled, waking me up in a state of panic. I didn't even remember falling asleep in the first place.

Blinking, I ignored the throbbing pain in the middle of my legs as I tried to focus on the woman standing in front of me. I knew damn well that Cree didn't fuck me in another bitch's house and then let my ass fall asleep. The light snapped on in the room, temporarily blinding me. Cree stirred, mumbled something under his breath right before she yelled again.

"Nigga, get the hell up!" she yelled.

"Oh my God!" I gasped when my eyes were able to adjust to the light. There was definitely another woman in the room and she looked mad as hell about me being there. But it wasn't anyone Cree was fucking with. It looked like his grandmother.

145

"Big Mama, what you trippin' for?" Cree mumbled, trying to cover his head with a pillow.

Frowning, his grandmother walked up on him, just as I scrambled to cover my naked body with the bed sheets, and snatched the pillow off his head.

"What I told you 'bout bringin' these random women by my fuckin' house?!" she cursed, and I felt like shit when she turned her glare on me.

Damn. She thought I was just any other hoe. But I couldn't blame her. Hell, that's what it looked like at the moment. Like I was some thot he found at the club and fucked in his grandma's spot.

"Big Mama, I pay for everything in this shit. Why you trippin'?" he fussed, finally deciding to sit up in the bed.

"Because I told you 'bout this shit! I don't care what you pay for. This is my damn house and I told you don't be bringin' no random hoes over here!"

Okay, she was old and I was raised to respect my elders but I wasn't about to be too many more hoes. It was time for me to get my shit and go before I told her ass that, too. Yeah, I was in her grandson's bed after only meeting him the day before, but so what? I still wasn't in the same category as some of the hood bunnies he could have been mixed up with.

"I'm out," I mumbled as I stood up, naked as the day that God gave me my first breath, and started looking for my clothes.

"Humph!" his grandmother grunted, hands on her hips as she eyed my body.

I wasn't bashful when it came to showing skin because I knew I was bad. I'd only covered up out of respect for her when she burst in the room. But at the moment, I really didn't give two fucks what she thought about me because it didn't matter. She came in thinking I was a hoe from jump so a hoe I would be. If she would step out of the way and let me get dressed, she wouldn't have to see me again.

"See? She goin'," Cree said to his grandmother. "Can you leave for a minute so she can get dressed?"

"Happily," she mumbled, shooting another glare at me before turning around and walking out the door. "Wit' her nasty, stankin' ass."

She was a bitch. And I know that sounds bad but she was! Never in my life would I have thought I'd say that about *anybody's* grandmother but that lady took me there! And she didn't even look like a grandmother, to be real. She looked like how Angela Basset would in about twenty more years. The lady had muscles and all hiding up under her housecoat... she looked like she could hold her own in the streets if it came down to it. I don't know why they called her 'Big Mama' because there was nothing big about her. Except her nasty ass attitude.

"You need me to give you a ride?" Cree asked and I shook my head.

"I can find my own way," I huffed as I snatched my dress up from off the floor.

"Here, I can give you a shirt and some basketball shorts so you don't have to put that back on. You can wear some of my slides too," he offered, standing up.

I didn't say anything but I was grateful for the offer. Last thing I wanted was to be walking down the street in my clothes from the previous night, letting everyone around know that I was fresh out of bed from a one-night stand.

"Here," Cree said, tossing me some clothes and I started to put them on without saying a single word. "My bad 'bout my Big Mama... she crazy sometimes."

"And mean as hell," I added under my breath, more to myself than him.

"What? You mean my sweet old grandma?" he asked, his tone dripping with sarcasm.

"You know what? Why would you even bring me here? Who has sex with somebody in their fuckin' grandma's house?" I asked, cutting my eyes at him.

Shrugging, he looked back at me and stood up, pushing his hands into the pockets of the sweatpants he'd put on at some point in the night.

"Ain't no other chick ever complained 'bout the shit," he explained.

"Oh? So they just like havin' your grandmother burst up in the room callin' them a hoe?" I countered with much attitude.

"Naw... It's never happened because I don't let them spend the night," he said and I paused, feeling the anger in me fall away a bit. "I always make them leave before she wakes up."

Something about the fact that he was admitting that he usually kicked chicks out but hadn't done it to me, made me feel some kind of way. But I pushed it away with a shrug. It didn't mean anything. Maybe he was too tired to make me leave. It could have been anything, and the last thing I wanted to do was read too much into things.

"Okay, I'm leaving. Thanks for the clothes," I told him and grabbed my clutch so I could walk out.

"Naw, I'mma drive you," he told me and I looked over as he pulled a black hoodie over his head.

I followed him out of the room and through the house. As soon as we walked through the living room, he paused so he could grab the keys off the counter and I felt his grandmother's eyes on me. Crossing my arms in front of my chest, I tried to ignore her.

"You ain't takin' my car!" she said just as Cree got the keys.

"Big Mama, what you mean?" he asked. "I bought you that car!"

"I don't care. It's bad enough you used it last night without askin'. You need to figure out another way to get your company home. She wasn't 'posed to be here any damn way," she muttered and I sucked my teeth.

I wasn't like Janelle. She was patient and slow to anger but I had an attitude… a bad one at that, and I didn't care to hide it either. His grandmother was testing the shit out of me because if she had been anyone else, I would have gone off on her ass.

"Let me walk you back," Cree mumbled, turning to me. "It's only a block over."

"Naw, you good."

Without saying a word, I took off ahead of him, unlocking the front door my damn self as I stomped off with my clothes, shoes and clutch in my hand. This was some bullshit, but I should have known that good dick came with problems. It always did.

Shame.

Outlaw

*J*anelle had some shit with her ass. I didn't know what kind of game she was playing but I was gonna figure it out.

She had some Dr. Jekyll and Mr. Hyde type shit going on. Like she was an uptight professional chick by day and 'freak fantastic' by night. After spending the night with her, I woke up to her nudging me hard in my side, telling me to get the hell out before Val woke up and caught me there.

My first thought was 'who gives a shit 'bout Val?'. I hadn't fucked her and she wasn't my bitch. I went out with her one time and, after finding out that she was Janelle's roommate, I only stayed out with her as long as I did to piss Janelle off. Val wasn't my type. She was too eager for attention and was willing to do anything for it. She was the type of chick who had lost herself looking for love. She was too eager to please to the point she didn't know who the hell she was… she became whatever and whoever the nigga with her wanted. I wasn't feelin' that shit.

But it didn't matter to Janelle because, in her mind, she had gone against some unspoken girlfriend code by being with me and didn't want anyone to find out.

"Aye, I wanna see you again, tho," I told her as she started throwing my clothes at me, urging me to get them on and get the hell out. Damn, she had me feeling like the bitch now. She was telling me to leave, forcing my ass out her shit, and I was pressing her to spend more time with my ass.

"Yeah… Okay, um…" she paused and crinkled her brows as if thinking about whether or not hanging with me again was a good deal.

What the fuck? I couldn't believe this shit. This girl had let me fuck, doing whatever I liked to every part of her body, but now she had to think about whether or not she wanted to see me again.

"Maybe we can… I just—I don't know. We can talk about it later," she said finally, sighing heavily. "But you have to go… now!"

Shaking my head, I started to get dressed, only putting on my sweats and black tee. She put her hand to her lips, telling me to quiet down but I wasn't trying to hear that shit. She wasn't telling a nigga to be quiet while I was all up in that pussy, fuckin' her so good that she was moaning all kinds of shit. We even got it in while in the shower which was right next to Val's room. She ain't say shit then either!

Stomping towards the door, I snatched the door open and took off down the hall, ignoring her hissing and whispers for me not to make so much noise. What the hell I looked like sneaking through a chick's house just so another chick, who I didn't fuck, wouldn't see me? She was on some lil' girl shit.

"Why are you actin' like this?!" she asked me, stopping me just as I got to the front door. I watched as she turned her head, checking down the hall to make sure Val wasn't up and that pissed me the fuck off.

"Because I'm a grown fuckin' man! And, on top of that, I didn't fuck her. She can't say shit to you because there ain't shit to say."

"It's not just that," she started, looking away as she paused.

Squaring my shoulders, I stood right in front of her and looked straight in her eyes.

"Then what is it?" I pushed, my agitation still coming through in my tone. I didn't like the position she was putting me in, making me feel like I was on some female type shit for wanting to deal with her.

"It's..." she sighed and looked over at some shit she had on the dining room table. It looked like some files and stuff she'd probably brought home from work. Then I went back to her face, instantly recognizing something in her expression.

"Oh... you're a good girl who just fucked a thug and it's got you thrown, huh?" I asked in a teasing way, although I was starting to get heated the more I thought about it. She was embarrassed by me and that's why she had woke me up early as hell to push my ass out the house. She didn't want anybody to know that I'd had sex with her.

When she couldn't meet my eyes, I knew I was right. I didn't need to hear anything further. In life, *no* bitch living had ever been ashamed to fuck around with me. I didn't care who she was. I'd fucked white girls, black girls, Asians, Hispanics... all kinds from all races and all backgrounds. And each one had been begging me to make shit with them official. But here she was dissin' a nigga just because she didn't want her friends knowing that we fucked around. She could get the fuck outta here with this bullshit.

"Move," I told her and she backed away from the door, keeping her head low.

Without saying anything else, I turned around, opened the door and walked out. I was mad as hell as I left her crib, hopping in my ride and speeding off without giving her ass a second glance.

Not Your Average Girl.

Sidney

"Girl, this nigga steady tellin' muthafuckas that this ain't his baby but he still slidin' through for the pussy whenever he get a chance. Ain't that some shit?" Faviola said as I laced up my sneaks.

"No, what's some shit is that fact that you keep lettin' that nigga slide through after talkin' reckless," I told her, dishing her some real shit that I knew she was gonna get an attitude about.

When I heard her suck her teeth, I knew I was right but I didn't care. I was the type of friend who said what you needed to hear even if you didn't want to, and it wasn't something I was trying to change just because Faviola was always in her feelings now that she was pregnant.

My name is Sidney and, yes, I am perfectly aware that it's a 'boy' name. I heard that shit all the time when I was younger. It also didn't help that I dressed and acted like a boy too. I was a through and through tomboy. I didn't own a single dress, a single pair of heels, and my favorite hairstyle was my neat ass ponytail that I'd perfected through the years. I was rough and always preferred to hang with the boys rather than the girls, which was the reason that I'd had multiple broken bones when I was younger, giving me a high tolerance for pain.

But don't get me wrong… yes, I was boyish but I was full woman on the inside and I loved men. I was not a lesbian, although I didn't see anything wrong with being a lesbian. In fact, one of my best friends was a lesbian. A fine one too… Sway was always bagging all the finest females wherever we went. She got more pussy than niggas from chicks who didn't even know they went that way until they saw her. People assumed that I was the same way because we hung together, but it wasn't true. I was into guys.

"I'm about to go play some ball," I told Faviola after getting my gear together. Walking into the closet, I grabbed my basketball and tossed my hoody over my head because it was kinda cold outside.

"Where? I thought you got fired from the gym?" she said, and I knew she was mentioning it to try and piss me off since she knew I was still mad about that shit.

I got fired from a job I'd had for years, on my fuckin' day off. And it was over some bullshit too. The new manager tried to push up on me and when I told her ass that I didn't chill with chicks like that, she found a way to get my ass fired.

"I'm goin' to the court," I told her as I shot by her to the front door.

She gave me a look but I ignored it and walked out before she could say anything. I knew exactly what her look was about and I didn't want to get into it. It had been a long time since I'd played basketball at the neighborhood court here in Brooklyn and there was a reason why. In fact, the only reason I'd even gotten the job at the gym was so I could play for free at that court in order to avoid this one. But, like I said, it had been years so I figured I needed to get over the past and get with the present.

About thirty minutes into a game with myself, I was just getting warmed up. The crisp, November air kept me from sweating and I was doing the damn thing, sinking baskets like I was made for the pros.

"Ain't see you out here in a minute," a voice said from behind me right when I was about to sink my next basket, which would have made it fifteen three-point shots in a row. But the sound of his voice threw me off and I wobbled right when I launched the ball, missing the shot.

Turning around, I looked right into his eyes, feeling all kinds of emotions that I couldn't explain.

Damn it, Sidney, I cursed myself as I stared at him.

I knew there was a good possibility that I'd see him out here but that's why I'd come out early, when the court was usually empty. I figured that there was no way I would run into him then. I also figured that the effect that he had on me was near its end.

After seeing him so often with other women, I just knew there was no way my emotions would allow me to feel a single thing for him. But standing there, staring into his beautiful brown eyes as he stood in front of me dressed simply in sweatpants and a hoody, I couldn't help but feel that familiar feeling stirring up in my chest. Then I made the mistake of looking down at the crotch of his sweatpants and saw that monster he was holding, pressed up against his thigh. Damn. I had it bad.

"Because I haven't been here in a minute," I replied back to him. "You know that."

Turning around, I ran to grab my ball and started back my game, ignoring him as much as I could, but my body was still reacting to his presence. He watched me for a while but then I saw as he dropped the basketball he was holding and started towards me. A feeling fell over me that I can't explain, as he came over and posted up behind me, jumping right into my game. It was like old times. Me and him on the court, playing the most sensuous and sexual game of basketball there ever was.

Every time I had the ball, he'd crouch down low behind me, thrusting his pelvis into my ass, giving me a feel of his rock hard erection. He knew I wanted him still. Even after everything we'd been through, he knew that I did and I always would.

But then he took it a step farther, just like I knew he would and grabbed me by my hips, pulling me close to him, as he gently pressed his lips against my neck. I began to panic when I felt the familiar feelings of passion come up in my chest, reminding me that he was doing it to me once again. He always did this to me and I hated him for it. I couldn't let it slide this time.

"Stop that shit!" I yelled, pushing him away. Whipping around, I glared into his eyes, noting the hurt in them. How dare he look at me that way? After years of hurting me, how dare he make feel bad for anything?

"What's wrong?" he asked, frowning as he stepped close to me. I held my hands out, pressing them against his chest to stop him from coming any closer.

"Don't play that shit with me," I told him, breathing heavily. "You know why I stopped coming here. You know why I stopped hanging around with you. You're always tryin' to fuck with me and you know I don't like that shit, Yolo!"

Okay, let me stop here and shed some light on my fucked up situation. I was hopelessly, ridiculously and secretly in love with one of the Murray brothers. The reason why it was a secret was not because of me. It was because of him.

When I was younger, Yolo and his brothers would come every summer to visit their grandmother and him and I would hang out. It started as just a friendship. He saw me as one of the boys, the same way that I saw myself. We would shoot hoops, smoke weed and get into whatever shit we could find until it was time to go home. A few nights, Yolo and I would even sneak out of the house to just hang out and chill. We were like best friends but that was it.

Until things changed.

Somewhere along the way, I fell in love with him. When I finally got the nerve to tell him, he confessed that he felt the same way about me too. We had snuck out the house to hang out together that night and after realizing how each other felt, we had sex for the first time. Well… it was my first time anyways.

After that, we kept our relationship secret but still messed around in private. I didn't know any better so I was cool with that. Until Yolo started messing with a girl named LaTrese. LaTrese was cool and I didn't have any issues with her until she started messing with Yolo, but I couldn't say anything about it because she didn't know what him and I had. But what really got me was that although Yolo kept our shit in private, everything he did with LaTrese was public knowledge. He made her his official girlfriend and paraded her around like she was a prize, while he still tried to keep everything secret with me.

Deep down I knew why. LaTrese was the girl everyone wanted. She was beautiful, had long hair and nice skin. She dressed nice as hell and was thick in all the right places. Who wouldn't want to claim her? I was most likely walking around looking like one of the boys, in shorts, sweats, and a tank top with some sneakers on. How could I compete?

Either way, he broke my heart, but I was in love so I continued dealing with him in secret, going along with the lie that what he had with LaTrese wasn't nothing compared to what we had. It wasn't until LaTrese became pregnant with his first child that I decided to cut it off for good and get a job at the gym so I wouldn't see him anymore when I played ball. Everything about the court reminded me of what we used to have, and I couldn't get over him as long as I practiced there.

LaTrese ended up losing the baby and Yolo tried to reach out to me so that I could help him through the tragedy of losing his son, but I refused to meet with him. Since then, we'd seen each other in passing at the club or in the hood, but we didn't talk. He continued to flip through chicks… all of them looked like model types, nothing like me. I knew everything that he was doing but I refused to be caught alone with him or to speak to him anymore. Until now.

"Sidney, don't be like that. You know I—"

"Just stop!" I told him, shaking my head.

The look in his eyes was hurting me to the core. He seemed stricken and confused, like he was really at a loss for why I was acting the way I was. Leave it to his ass to act this way. The nigga was on his way to getting an MD but he couldn't understand the bullshit actions that led us to this point.

"I'm gonna go," I said finally, realizing that I wasn't strong enough to push him away for long. If Yolo wanted me, he would have me and that was it. My resolve was breaking and I just needed to go.

"I can't be around you anymore. Just leave me the fuck alone."

Running to the side of the court, I grabbed my ball and turned to leave. Before I could walk by him, Yolo reached out and grabbed my hand, stopping me from going any further.

"Sidney, man, listen... I'm not the same nigga I was back then," he started, licking his lips and I felt myself get weak as hell.

All of the Murrays were fine but Yolo was, hands down, the sexiest of them all. Maybe I was biased but I didn't think so. Yolo was light-skinned, straight yellow, which of course is how he got his name. He had the sexiest, droopy eyes and the plumpest, suckable lips I'd ever seen. He wasn't thin built like Cree, but he wasn't real thick and wide like Tank either. He was just right, perfectly in the middle.

"I've been giving you your space but I don't know if I want to do that anymore," he said, bringing his eyes up to meet mine. Looking at the only man I'd ever loved, I wanted so badly to just cave in and give him what he wanted but I couldn't.

And yes, I know it seems like he's being genuine, but you don't know Yolo like I do. This is not the first time he's made it seem like he wanted to get it right and be with only me. In fact, he'd given me a speech like this right before LaTrese's ass popped up pregnant!

"That's bullshit, Yolo, and you know it. You haven't been giving me space. You've been doing you," I told him, nudging his hand from my arm. "And you can keep doing you because I'm not falling for it."

"I love you, Sidney," he told me and my heart broke into a million pieces and scattered across the floor.

"No you don't, Yolo. You never did," I declared, telling him my honest thoughts. Then I pushed away from him and ran away, hoping that he couldn't see me wiping the tears from my face.

Pride.

Janelle

I knew I hurt Luke's feelings but I didn't have the slightest idea as to how to fix it. Or even if I should. Well, I guess it doesn't matter whether I should or not because I definitely wanted to. Problem is… I never did what I wanted to do. I always did what I should do—which is why I hadn't even tried to call him and apologize.

"Hello?" I answered the phone with a smile, happy to be speaking to the one man who never let me down.

"Hey baby, I hope you and Carmella aren't having too much fun. I spoke with her earlier and she said she's been studying during her break. For some reason, I'm almost positive that's not true."

Instead of answering my father, I giggled my reply, knowing that he already knew the truth about that. Since when did Carmella ever study over a break? She barely studied when she wasn't on break.

"We're being safe. That's all I'll say," I teased and he chuckled in response.

"I'll take that. How's Old Pelmington treating you? He letting you first chair any major cases yet?" my daddy asked and I swear I could almost see his grin just by hearing the warmth in his voice.

"If by that you mean is he letting me swim through his old stuff and pretend to be in charge, then yes," I replied, rolling my eyes.

"Just stick with it. It'll all be worth it in the end," he instructed, repeating one of his favorite lines that I'd probably heard every day of my life growing up. It was his motto. I didn't even have to answer him because he knew I would. I was just like him... I never gave up.

"So enough of that," he said, his tone dropping. "Any new prospects on the horizons? You not getting any younger and I would like to see you married and happy while I can still enjoy my grandkids."

I giggled again at the thought of my daddy being a grandfather. It just didn't seem like it fit. He was in his fifties and looked better than men half his age. Sporting a muscular build, he was tall, dark and gorgeous, even if I do say so myself.

"Um..." I began, stalling when I really thought about his question. The answer was that I definitely had found someone to pique my interest but there was no way I could ever tell him about Luke.

"Yes..." I continued, biting the inside corner of my mouth. "His name is... Chris Harvaty and he works with me."

There was a slight pause and I felt my heart twinge in my chest at telling my father a lie. I mean... it wasn't a complete lie, right? I definitely liked Chris.

"Harvaty? Is he from Nebraska? Is his mother—"

"Yes," I answered rolling my eyes as a smile came across my face. Chris thought his mother's reputation hadn't spread outside of Nebraska but obviously he was wrong.

"Wow... I can't wait to meet him," my daddy said, shocking me to the point that my mouth dropped open. *Meet* him? Who said anything about *meeting* anyone?

"Bring him with you when you come home for Thanksgiving. I've heard a lot about his family and would love for him to join us... if he can make it, that is," he added and I tried to swallow the lump in my throat so that I could respond.

"I—I will ask him."

Closing my eyes, I took a deep breath and then muddled through the rest of the conversation with my dad as I walked down the street towards my apartment. To be honest, my heart wasn't in it. Once again, I felt like I was making a decision that wasn't based off the things I wanted or myself. But, in the end, I knew that I was doing what was right. And doing what was right had worked out well for me so far, right?

Just as I was walking up the steps of my building, Carmella called and I stopped to pull out my keys and answer her call.

"Hey, I'm going to be in late tonight," Carmella announced as I fumbled with my keys.

"Late? Like how late?"

"Too late for you to wait up for me. It'll be pass your bedtime, grandma, so just leave the key out for me," she told me and I rolled my eyes. What was wrong with getting a decent night's sleep when you knew you had to work early in the morning? Why did that have to make me a grandma?

"Okay," I told her as I opened up the door. "I'll leave it under the—"

Seeing who was standing in front of me, my sentence cut short and my mouth fell open. I nearly dropped my bags from my arms too, as I struggled to get myself together.

"Bye," I told Carmella, hanging up the phone before narrowing my eyes on the person standing in my kitchen with a t-shirt and boxers on. "What are you doing here?"

And no, it was not Luke standing there in front of me waiting for me to come home. That would have been too good to be true, right? Well, turns out it was because, instead of Luke, it was the guy from the club. The one I'd been dancing with right before Luke came over and kicked his ass out.

"Aye, I ain't kno' you lived here," he said, his eyes lowering as he took in my appearance. "Damn, you look different from the other night but still fine as hell."

Unmoving, I stood in the same spot with my hand still holding the handle of the door.

"I said, what are you doing here?" I repeated, more firmly than before.

"Chill," he told me, putting his hands up. "I'm here because I was invited here. I'm chillin' wit' Val."

What the hell? I was pissed. Slamming the door closed behind me, I gritted my teeth together to try to stop myself from going off. It was bad enough that Val was always bringing some unknown niggas into the apartment without telling me, but now she was bringing someone in who was mixed up in some shit with Luke that I wanted no parts with.

Ignoring him, I walked down the hall and to my room, pushing the door closed behind me. I really couldn't take this shit anymore. I needed to move. I liked Val as a person but there was just some things I couldn't get with, and this was one of them. She just couldn't keep her damn legs closed and I didn't feel safe in my own house.

I was getting undressed when I began to feel uneasy. Bending over, I pulled my shorts up over my thighs and glanced at the door, noticing that it was partially open. I pulled the shorts on over my ass and stood up to go press it closed, but stopped when I saw a pair of eyes looking back at me.

"What the fuck are you doing looking inside my room?!" I yelled, pulling the door all the way open. I was so mad that I didn't even care that I was standing there, wearing only a bra.

"Chill... I was just gettin' a look, ma. You look good as hell. You wanna join us or you still fuckin' with that nigga, Outlaw?" he asked and I glared at him with wide-eyes, totally unbelieving his nerve.

"You need to get the fuck out!" I screamed. He leaned forward like he was going to grab me and before I knew it, I'd reached back and slapped the shit out of him.

His eyes flared and Val opened the door to her room, stepping out while rubbing her eyes and yawning as if she had been sleep. Perfect. She had some nasty ass nigga that I was sure she barely knew, walking around our apartment while she was sleeping in the room.

"Brandon... What the hell is going on?" she asked, frowning at me as I stood at my door in shorts and a bra.

"He needs to get the hell out of here! He was staring at me while I was getting undressed!" I yelled, pointing my finger at the guy who I now knew was named Brandon. Stepping back, he looked at me with a frown on his face as if I was lying.

"Naw, ma, don't lie. You on dat bullshit because you kno' dat ain't how dat shit happened. You left the door open and waited for a nigga to come down the hall before you started bootin' ya ass in the air and shit—"

"WHAT?!" I barked, glaring at him. Did I just hear this nigga right?

"Don't act like that now. She was in the kitchen tryin' to throw her pussy at me... I saw her in the club the other night and she tried to get at me but I wasn't feelin' that shit. Now you wanna act like a nigga tried you. Ma, I ain't never been thirsty behind no bitch!"

Reaching back, I was about to slap the shit out of him again but Val stepped in the way and pushed me back hard.

"Keep your fuckin' hands off him!" she yelled at me and I had to do a double-take. She had to be kidding right now. Was she really about to take his side over mine?

"Val, you can't possibly believe his ass! You barely know him!"

Rolling her eyes, Val sucked her teeth and narrowed her eyes at me.

"Don't even start with that bullshit, Janelle. It's not like you ain't come on to someone that I brought home before! I saw who you had in here the other night! You be actin' all goody-goody but as soon as I dropped Luke, here you go fuckin' him!"

Shit... how the hell did she find out I had Luke in here?

"That is not how it happened, Val!" I yelled back at her. "I knew

Luke from—"

"I don't give a fuck where you knew him from!" she spat, looking at me with her nose curled up like something stunk. "You're nothing but a self-righteous bitch! Always walking around here like your shit don't stank but I finally see you for who you are. All you want is my fuckin' life! Leave me the fuck alone!"

Frowning, I was at a loss for words as I stared at the look on Val's face. The bitch was delusional. With all her trips to the clinic and the pharmacy to clean up her little mistakes, how the hell could I want her life? Maybe it was because I was mad as hell or maybe it was because I'd finally got some dick in my life… I didn't know what it was but, for some reason, I wasn't ready to back down and let her think I wanted anything concerning her.

"Val, why the hell would I want your fuckin' life? Your ass stay in the clinic getting rid of shit that you catch from these niggas you keep letting run through you! Does Brandon know that I just went to the pharmacy to pick you up a prescription for—"

Val's fist came across my face so fast that I couldn't see for a minute. It was like my brain needed a second to catch up with what was happening. Then I started throwing punches, trying to connect with whatever I could as Val threw them right back at me. She grabbed onto my hair and that's when I went wild, biting my lip and throwing punches upwards as she snatched so hard, I knew that she'd tore a few strands loose.

"ARGH!" she screamed and I felt sticky, wet liquid on my fist. She released my hair and I backed up, rubbing the spot that stung the most.

"You broke my nose!" she yelled at me as she held onto her face, blood covering most of her face. Her nose didn't look broken but it was definitely bleeding really bad. Instantly, I began to feel bad for what I'd done. I really hadn't meant to hurt her.

"Val, I'm so sorry. I—"

"GET THE FUCK AWAY FROM ME, BITCH!" she screamed just as I reached out to help her. "I hate you! Don't fuckin' touch me!"

And with that, she stormed in the room, leaving me and Brandon standing in the hallway. Turning, he began to walk behind her to the room, stopping only for a second to toss me a taunting smile. Backing into my room, I slammed the door closed and locked it before walking to my mirror to check for bruising.

This was it between me and Val. I definitely had to get out.

Stalker.

Outlaw

"Aye, this your car now, nigga," I said, tossing Cree the keys to my whip. Grabbing the keys, he frowned at them before looking up at me.

"What da hell you on right now, nigga?" he asked, laughing before he tossed the keys right back at me. "I know you ain't givin' nobody yo' shit. You just bought it."

Walking over, I sat down between him and Tank, shaking my head. We were about to get started on our poker game but my mind wasn't in it. This poker game was only for my brothers and I because we had business to discuss. It looked like them niggas had already started drinking and shit before I got there.

"Man… I let a chick ride in it. In the front seat," I told them, and they understood immediately what I was saying. Frowning, I pulled out a small bag of weed and set it on the table, waiting for them to start with the bullshit.

"Hell naw, Outlaw," Tank started, turning all the way around in his seat so that he could look at me. "You tellin' me you let somebody ride up front in the whip? Naw, I kno' that's not what your ass is sayin'."

"Nigga, she tricked me. Let's get this game started. I'mma need these chips since I'm 'bout to have a baby on the way."

"Naw, she ain't trick yo' ass," Tank said with a smile on his face as he started shuffling the cards in his hands. "You must be in love wit' this chick to let that happen. When we gon' meet her?"

"Nigga, don't get fucked up in this bitch," I warned him, shooting him a look, but he only kept grinning at me. "Like I said, she tricked my ass. I wanted to take her home so I could hit it but she wouldn't get in the back."

"Wait... so did you hit?" Yolo asked and they all looked at me, everyone pausing as they waited for me to reply.

Frowning, I cut my eyes at Yolo. "Hell yeah, nigga. What da fuck you think my name is? Bitches can't resist this shit."

"Damn!" Cree said, laughing as he stood up with his drink in his hand. "Then let's toast to Outlaw and his baby mama!"

The only one who didn't move to make the toast was Kane, but I was used to that because he rarely joined in on the teasing and bullshit that my brothers and I did. Kane was always all business. Tank and Yolo all lifted their red cups like they were about to really toast that shit and I stood up, interrupting them as I swatted all their cups away.

"Nope. Slow y'all asses down. Ain't gon' be no baby because you kno' a nigga stays strapped up. Ain't tryin' to bless no bitch wit' my seed," I informed them as I started to roll up.

"Bless? Nigga, you mean 'curse,'" Tank chuckled as he laughed into his cup, taking a sip. "Ain't nobody ready to have a baby from yo' crazy ass. You'd be da fuckin' baby daddy from hell. Thinkin' you own her or some shit just because she got ya kid."

"Damn right," I agreed, nodding my head.

"Aye, you talkin' 'bout da chick from the club?" Cree asked. "Her sister the one I left wit'? I thought you said you wasn't feelin' her like that."

"I ain't," I told him with a shrug.

"Well, you better start, bruh," Yolo teased. "Because her ass 'bout to be your baby mama."

"Shut da fuck up, nigga!" I snapped, punching Yolo in his side as he laughed.

"How 'bout y'all all shut da fuck up? We got business to discuss," Kane started, his tone growing serious.

We all sat down in our chairs and got quiet as we waited for the oldest of us all to start. Tank shuffled the cards one last time and started to deal. Cree and Yolo sat, watching Kane intently as I pulled out my phone, checking my messages. I heard Kane clear his throat so I locked it and stuffed it in my pocket.

"First line of business I want to start wit' is dat fuck shit you pulled at the club the other night, nigga."

Kane furrowed his brow at me with a hint of contempt, and I felt a flare of anger rise up in me. I knew he was about to get in my ass and I hated that shit. Kane was always on me 'bout something and it never failed.

"What?!" I snapped after he just looked at me for a few minutes without saying a word. "What, I'm 'posed to guess what da hell you got on yo' mind?" I felt a bit of an adrenaline rush, like when something was about to pop off, and my mind and body was preparing for it.

"Don't fuckin' 'what' me, nigga! You know you just escaped a life sentence but you go and do some stupid shit like pull a fuckin' gun in the middle of the club," he admonished, glaring at me. "We just got yo' ass out and you know they just waitin' for any reason to bring you back in. They was tryin' to get us all locked up behind some shit you caused!"

Licking my lips, I tried to calm my nerves and not go to that place of no return as rage began to tug at my resolve. Nothing good would come out of this if I lost my anger; after all, this was my oldest brother but again, his mouth was on some reckless shit that I ain't like.

We locked eyes and the moment lingered with an imminent threat like a lull before the storm. But I was determined to bridle my anger and use diplomacy as he continued to stare holes into me. With a deep sigh, I plowed straight ahead, prepared to engage him as a palm of smoke from my blunt rose from the card table, enveloping us in its murky haze.

"Yo, check this. I feel what you sayin', bruh, but ain't no point in sayin' it. B came through knowin' what fuckin' time it was. He know I don't fuck wit' his ass after findin' out he was nothin' but a bitch. I took a charge for murkin' a nigga that he should've bodied as soon as he heard what he did to his fuckin' sister," I stubbornly told Kane, crossing my arms in front of my chest as my other brothers watched with the tension building, volatile like a stack of dynamite about to explode.

From just the silence and the sudden sober expressions on my brothers' faces, it was obvious they knew something was possibly about to get started. And as soon as I established eye contact with my older brother, Kane, I saw it smoldering in his eyes, as the right side of his face began to involuntarily twitch. That happens only when he is angry and doing a terrible job of controlling his temper.

Finally, he stood, impassive, and glowered at me with a cold steel look in his dark brown eyes as his face began to twitch more. Then he walked up on me and I braced myself. I could hear the scrape of chairs moving across the floor as my brothers moved about, as if to give us space. I tensed up, immediately wanting to go off on that nigga, but my oldest brother had whooped my ass enough times for me to think twice.

"You gotta learn to think wit' yo' fuckin' brain and save all that gangsta shit when you in public. You got niggas turnin' rat left and right and you givin' they asses somethin' to tell, wit'cho stupid ass—"

"Yo! Yo! Chill, nigga," I warned gesturing with my hand. There was grit in my voice. My anger was steadily increasing with each second. "I ain't tryin' to do this shit wit' you today, Kane."

"What, you gettin' mad, son?" he egged on, a hint of a humor at the end of his tone, like he was mocking me. "Huh, son? You gettin' mad?" he asked again, pushing me against my head and that's when I spazzed out.

"I'm not yo' fuckin' son!" I shouted, my attitude set on go. This was how it always was with me and Kane. I don't know why he was always riding my ass but I fuckin' hated that shit. It was like he deliberately tried to get a rise out of me each chance he got.

Jumping up with my fists in my side, I bumped chests with him, ready to go. Cree, Tank and Yolo all stared up at us, not saying a word as they watched on because they were used to me and Kane going at it. He was always on me about shit, trying to make me seem like the fuck up of the crew.

Suddenly, before I could even open up my mouth to say a single word, Kane reared back and punched me hard right in the gut.

"Fuck!" Cree yelled, jumping up as I doubled over and tried to catch my breath. The nigga had knocked the wind out my damn lungs.

"Watch yo' fuckin' mouth, nigga!" he yelled, before pulling me up just to punch my ass in the gut again. I swear I could feel his knuckles crush against my ribs.

Wheezing, I dropped to my knees and grabbed the back of the chair I'd been sitting in. My head was bowed down as I knelt on the floor, looking like I was praying. The way that nigga hit my ass, I should've been praying. Damn!

"Cree, get dat nigga in the fuckin' chair so we can discuss shit. You gone learn some fuckin' respect, Outlaw, and that's some real shit! You always doin' shit without thinkin' 'bout how your actions affect the rest of the fuckin' crew, but you gone fuckin' learn! We ain't work this hard for yo' unthinkin' ass to take us down!"

"Man, fuck you!" I yelled, even though Cree was telling me under his breath to just shut up and sit in my seat. Naw, Kane was tryin' the hell outta me and I wasn't having it. Standing up, I grabbed my gun out and held it to my side. I knew damn well I wasn't going to shoot Kane, just like everyone else in the room, but he had me heated to the point that I'd grabbed it out of habit.

"Fuck *me*?! And what? Now you wanna shoot me, huh?" Kane

started, squinting as he looked at me. "You gon' shoot me, Luke?"

"Man, y'all need to chill. This shit goin' too fuckin far," Tank said, standing up as Yolo and Cree nodded their heads in agreement. Clenching my jaw, I pushed my gun back into the waist of my jeans, not keeping my eyes off Kane. He stared at me for a moment, almost as if he were seeing something in me for the first time before beginning to speak.

"Nigga, get yo' ass in the fuckin' chair so we can discuss business. You mad disrespectful, yo. You think that you can do whatever the fuck you want but you bringin' unnecessary heat on us, fam. We got enough as it is. *Think*," he said, knocking his finger against his temple. "You wanna talk 'bout how you not my son but I'm the nigga always takin' care of ya ass when you get hemmed up in some bullshit, ain't I? Get ya fuckin' mind right."

Biting down on my back teeth, I listened to what he was saying as everyone waited for me to sit down. Deep down, I knew that Kane was right. He was always right, but it didn't mean I had to go for that shit just because everybody else did. Out of all my brothers, I was the only one to ever speak up against Kane. The rest of them just did whatever he said because he was the oldest but that was never me. If I had an issue with somethin', I was gonna state it and I didn't care who you were.

"C'mon, sit down, bruh," Cree said, trying to get me to my seat but I swatted his hand away. I ain't need him trying to help me sit down like I was a bitch.

Scowling, I grabbed my chair and sat in it, not saying shit but glaring at Kane the entire time. He looked back at me, unmoved by the look in my eyes.

"Now that we got that lil' shit out the way," he started, cutting his eyes at me and pausing as if daring me to say something. "We can move on to the important thing. Let's discuss this next hit."

***

"Where are we going? We just passed by here," Gina whined, making me realize that she was in the car with me. I'd been so focused on what I was doing, I had really forgotten she was sitting there.

Ignoring her, I didn't say a word. If anyone asked me what I was doing at the moment, I would lie my ass off. I hadn't heard from Janelle in over a week and, as much as I wanted to be mad at her, a nigga was missing her ass. I didn't just say that though.

Gina was my way of getting revenge on Janelle in my own way, I guess. She was a lawyer chick but she was older than Janelle and had been practicing for a while. I started messing with her a while back after meeting with her, when I was looking for someone to represent my brothers and I whenever we ran into some bullshit.

After Janelle kicked me out of her crib, making it seem like I wasn't good enough to be with someone like her, I called up Gina and she was happy as hell to hear from me. The whole reason I'd stopped messing with her was because she had started pressing me for a relationship, but I wasn't ready to go there with her.

But what annoyed the shit out of me was that Gina was sexy as hell, intelligent, successful, and had a daddy who was a judge but she didn't give a fuck about all that when it came to me. If I wanted to make things work with her, she would do it without thinking about what everybody else thought—including her husband. But Janelle ain't even come with all the shit Gina did and still wanted to act like she was too good for a nigga. That was some bullshit.

"And here we go again… are you lost?" Gina asked, staring out the window.

"I'm lookin' for somethin'," I told her as I circled around to drive by Janelle's job one more time. I glanced at the clock on the dash, noting that she should have been walking out any time now.

Sure enough, just as I was about to turn the corner, I saw Janelle walk out with that pretty nigga she was pretending that she liked. Stepping on the gas, I sped around the corner quick so that I could come back through and see what she was up to. Yeah, I was on that crazy shit, huh? But she was the one making me crazy. For real… I wouldn't have been down here trying to look for her but Gina's job was close to Janelle's so I figured 'why not?'.

When I pulled up, I saw Janelle crossing the street while holding hands with the pretty dude, and I instantly got heated. I slid to the side of the road and watched her, walking with him with a smile on her face as he talked on and on about some stupid shit.

Watching them got me heated to the max because I had never had no shit like this happen to me before. Never had I tried to show a female some attention only to have her reject it for a lame. That shit had me in my feelings.

"Let's go," I said, stepping out of the car. I had just seen them walk into a bar across the street and I was about to bust up all that shit.

"Huh?" Gina snapped right before I slammed the door in her face. She got out of the back of my car and I heard her heels clicking on the asphalt as she sprinted to catch up with me.

"Outlaw, what the hell are you up to? I saw you lookin' at that bitch." She sucked her teeth and I looked at her like she was crazy.

"You shouldn't give a fuck who I'm lookin' at!" I reminded her of her place quick.

She had a husband at home, probably waiting for her to bring her ass, but she was riding with me, steady telling me that if I wanted her, she would drop his ass without thinking twice. That was part of the reason I couldn't deal with her on no real level. She was disloyal as fuck.

"I'm just sayin'," she continued whining. "It wouldn't hurt you to have some respect. You asked me to ride with you."

Ignoring her, I walked cross the street as she clicked her heels right behind me. When I got into the restaurant, my eyes immediately began to search for Janelle. She was sitting at the bar, her fist under her chin as she gazed at the lil' light-skinned nigga in her face like she was feeling every word he was saying. But I knew better.

"Table for two?" a white chick asked, making me look at her for the first time.

"Yeah," I told her. "Lemme sit over at that table."

She nodded her head, smiled brightly, and led the way over to the table that I'd pointed at.

"I really want to sit at a booth," Gina whined from behind me.

"Ain't none."

"Yes, there are. Right over—"

"We good," I said, stopping the hostess. My eyes were still on Janelle and I was making sure that we were being seated right in her line of vision.

"Here are your menus. Your server will be here in just a minute," the woman said, giving us another smile but I just wanted her to move out the damn way.

"Oh! This is a nice place," Gina gushed, running her eyes over the menu.

She kept rattling on about all the stuff she wanted to order and how good everything sounded but I tuned her out. Eyes on Janelle, I focused my attention on her until, finally, she turned and looked right into my eyes. Her face dropped and she did a double-take. I could see her tense up as she tried to bring her attention back to pretty boy, obviously seeming uneasy knowing that I was there.

"That's right. I'm 'bout to break all that shit up," I muttered under my breath.

"What?" Gina asked, her greedy ass not even taking a second to look away from the menu.

"Nothin'," I replied, squinting my eyes at Janelle who seemed to be trying to explain to pretty boy about why she was all of a sudden sweating like a pig. Then she got up and took off towards the restrooms and I couldn't help but want to laugh. I had her ass shook.

"I'll be back," I said to Gina. She mumbled something but kept on staring at the menu.

Following behind Janelle, I pushed right into the women's bathroom, not giving a single fuck that it was another lady in there with her. Both of them turned and gawked at me as I walked in, stepping past the white lady to stand right in front of Janelle.

"What are you doing in here?!" the white lady gasped, placing her hand to her chest. I squinted at her, feeling like she looked familiar. Then her voice dropped.

"I paid the other one... Yolo. I paid him for everything last week," she whispered, as she looked at me from under her eyelids. Janelle turned and squinted at the woman.

"Oh shit... naw, you good," I told her with a small nod. She let out a breath of relief and then finished drying her hands before walking out of the bathroom. I locked the door as soon as she walked out.

"Why are you here?" Janelle asked just as I turned around to look at her. "You know you can't be—"

"I can't be here," I finished for her. "Because you don't wanna let nobody know that you fuckin' with an outlaw, huh?"

She rolled her eyes. "Don't try to be cute, Luke," she said, pursing her lips but I could tell that she liked it. "I can't do this with you... it was a mistake."

"A mistake," I repeated, narrowing my eyes. "So you tryin' to erase that mistake by dealin' with Pretty Boy out there?"

Sighing, Janelle looked everywhere but in my eyes. She crossed her arms in front of her chest and I couldn't ignore the fact that she looked damn good to me right then. She was on her professional shit but something about her had changed. She was bolder... sexier. She didn't seem like the little boring lawyer chick that she had been before. The perfect little daddy's girl who did everything the right way.

Crazy shit, huh? All she needed was to get some of this thug dick in her life and it turned her into another damn person.

"He's a good guy and I like him," she told me and I had to laugh.

"You say that shit like you're tryin' to convince yourself. I see through all that bullshit, Janelle. I *know* you," I told her and she shot her eyes at me, frowning like she had an attitude.

"You don't know me!"

"Oh yeah?" I asked with a smirk and, before she could say a single thing, I reached under her skirt and pushed it up.

She moved like she wanted to stop me but, in the end, didn't do a damn thing. I slipped a finger inside of her panties and watched her close her eyes as she enjoyed the feeling of me pushing inside of her. Fuck... she was so wet and it was about to drive my ass fuckin' crazy.

I pulled my finger out of her pussy and it made a smacking sound. Shit! I couldn't take it anymore. Grabbing her around the waist, I lifted her up and placed her on the sink, pushing her thighs open. My heart was beating hard in my chest because I knew I was about to do some shit that I'd never done before. But it was something I needed. In that moment, I felt like I needed to taste her.

Dropping to my knees, I pulled out my dick and started stroking it as I leaned over and started French kissing the hell out of her pussy, making sloppy sounds like I was hungry. Hell, I was. In that instance, it was like I was doing shit automatically... without even thinking about it. All I knew was that I wanted to taste her so badly and so I did.

"Ohhhh," she moaned, her thighs quivering as she continued to gush out more of her nectar. I sucked it up like the honey it was, greedily pulling her closer to me with one hand palming her ass. She began to rotate her hips against my face and I pushed my tongue in even further, closing my eyes as she fucked my face. I moved my head side-to-side, using my nose to flick at her clit as I shoved my tongue down her hole, fucking her back.

"Fuuuuuck," she murmured as precum ran down my fingers. I couldn't hold back anymore.

Standing up, I licked my lips and then pushed her thighs open, entering her swiftly. I pulled her forward so that she was off-balance and fell into me as I fucked her hard, ramming my dick straight through her. Fuck... I didn't have on a rubber but my mind wasn't even on it. I'd worry about that later.

"Shit... I'm 'bout to cum, baby," she moaned in my ear, gripping my back hard as I fucked her into ecstasy. I felt myself about to cum too and I bit my lip, knowing that I was going to have to pull out but it was just too fuckin' hard.

"Let me swallow it," she muttered, knowing what was about to happen. Damn... that was music to my ears.

"Okay," I told her and pulled out. She dropped to her knees and went to work, sucking and deepthroating me fast as I bit down hard on my tongue to stop myself from crying out like a little bitch.

"SHIT!" I cursed, looking down at her while I came. She sucked it down, slurping and stroking my meat with one hand as she swallowed every bit of the nut.

Fuck it. I was in love.

"You good?" she asked me, teasing the head of my dick with the tip of her tongue. She had changed. I'm telling you. She wasn't the same chick that I'd met before.

"Let me find out you a fuckin' freak," I told her, smirking as I fixed up my clothes and helped her stand to her feet. She only smiled and started fixing her skirt. Then, suddenly, her face dropped.

"Shit! I forgot about Chris!"

She turned around and started washing her hands, running water over her face while I watched her. She had just swallowed my seed and now she was worried about the next nigga.

"Tell that nigga you babysittin'," I told her and she frowned at me, confused.

"Babysittin'?" she asked and I smirked. "I'm not—"

"Yeah you are. You got a whole bunch of my shorties in ya belly right now. Tell that nigga you busy."

She looked like she was about to be pissed off for a minute and then shook her head.

"No, what I'm about to do is go out there and finish up my date while you finish yours because *this*…" she pointed between her and I. "…was never supposed to happen."

"Well, *this*…" I pointed between the two of us, mocking her. "… was what you wanted to happen. Don't play dumb now because I can see through that bullshit. I didn't make you take the dick and you not 'bout to be chillin' wit' dat nigga no more."

"Yes, I am!" she spat, crossing her arms in front of her chest. "You don't tell me what to do!"

She licked her lips and I had a flashback to how it was wrapped around my dick just seconds ago. And now she wanted to go and chill with another nigga. Not happening.

"Fuck outta here wit' dat bullshit, yo! I ain't gon' tell you dis shit again. End that fuckin' date or it's gon' be me, you and that nigga sittin' and talking shit together!"

Janelle snarled at me, the edges of her lips pulled up as she stared into my eyes like she hated me.

"You showed up here with another woman and now you wanna tell me what to do?" she started and I shrugged. "Oh really? You think that's okay? Well, you get rid of her and I'll get rid of Chris."

"Fine," I said with ease.

I wasn't really feeling Gina like that no way. She had a man, and I didn't want to deal with her constantly asking for me to make things official with her ass.

"Fine," she said and then stomped over to the bathroom door, unlocked it and walked out.

Satisfied with my win, I glanced in the mirror to make sure I was on point, before walking out a few seconds after her. When I got to the table, Gina was pissed off to the max, sipping on a drink as she held her face in her hand and glared at me.

"Have fun?" was all she said because she knew better than to question me about what I'd been doing. Plus, I was sure she already knew.

"Yeah," I replied as I watched Janelle talking to Pretty Boy. She was obviously coming up with some lie as to why she had to go and I couldn't hide my smile when I saw her grab her purse and walk away.

"Let's go," I told Gina, standing up, my eyes still planted on the door that Janelle had just walked out of.

"What you mean?" she asked with an attitude. "I didn't even get to eat yet!"

"I did."

The Glow Up.

Carmella

"Turn that shit up! That's my song!" I yelled right when I heard a Beyoncé song come on.

I was in the car with a group of friends… well, I had really only met them over the few days I'd been in New York visiting Janelle, but they were fun as hell. One was her neighbor, Sidney, and the other was Sidney's friend, Faviola, who was pregnant. Her ass wasn't showing a bit but she did not miss any opportunity to let everyone know she was holding a baby in her damn stomach. I liked her though.She was cute as hell but had that ghetto swag that made her seem real as hell. She called herself the Black Barbie but she ain't look like any Barbie I'd ever seen… unless Barbie had a hood ass Brooklyn version I never seen.

We also had Sway in the car with us. She reminded me of Snoop, from *The Wire*. She was a dyke and cool as hell with it, super laid back. Initially, I thought that her and Sidney was a couple, but Sidney quickly informed me that she was not gay, even though she dressed like a nigga half the time. Her ass stayed in some sweats or basketball shorts, a t-shirt and some Jordans. It's like it was all she owned.

"Naw, turn that shit down. I don't like that bitch!" Sidney yelled, smiling, so I knew she was really teasing me.

"Who doesn't like Beyoncé? Your ass is a hater!" I shouted back, leaning into the front of the car so I could turn the song up.

"Yeah, my ass is hatin'," Sidney said, laughing. "I love this damn song."

Sway drove through Brooklyn as me, Sidney and Faviola sang "Sorry" to the top of our lungs, making motions with our hands just like we were in the video. Then I looked out the window and saw someone that I recognized walking on the side of the road.

"Sway, slow down!" I yelled over the music and rolled down the window, looking right at Cree's fine ass.

So remember when I said that good dick came with bullshit? Well, it did. It always did. But at the end of the day, it was *still* good dick! That said, yes, I was still messing around with Cree's punk ass.

"Aye!" I yelled, hanging out the window, with my elbows keeping my balance.

I waited for Cree to turn towards me and greeted him with two middle fingers, making Sidney, who was watching me, laugh her ass off. He shook his head and said something under his breath, pulling his headphones from his ears.

"Hey, y'all, I'mma come through and hang later," I told them as I grabbed my bag and opened up the car door.

"Mmhmm," Sidney teased, smiling at me. "Gon' head and hang with yo' boo, girl."

"Yep, and make a baby so our kids can be cousins," Faviola added, rubbing on her flat ass belly.

I rolled my eyes. She was happy as hell that Cree's older brother,

Tank, had knocked her ass up. From what Sidney had told me, she had trapped him too. She hit him with one of the oldest tricks in the book… offered him a condom that she'd poked a hole in, and the nigga went for that shit.

Sway sped off as I walked over slowly to Cree, taking all of him in with my eyes. He was fine as hell to me, even though I couldn't get over his attitude. He just didn't treat me like I was used to niggas treating me. I was used to them falling all over me, eager to please and do whatever I wanted, but he wasn't the type.

"Where you comin' from?" he asked, looking down the road at the car I'd gotten out of with a crazy look on his face.

"From hangin' wit' my girls. Why?" I asked, frowning, as I placed my hand on my hip.

"I don't want you hangin' wit' that Flavor Flave chick," he told me and my frown deepened with confusion.

"You mean Faviola?" I asked, correcting him as I tilted my head to the side.

"Yeah, her. She bad news," he added before turning around to keep walking down the street.

"Well, I'll keep that in mind for when you become my man and you can tell me who to not hang with," I shot back, sucking my teeth. Cree cut his eyes at me but didn't say anything so we walked on in silence.

"You wanna go out with me tonight? Like, round eight?" he asked me all of a sudden and I stopped to look at him.

"Go out? In what car? Your grandma's?" I inquired with attitude, placing my hands on my hips. Turning to me, he screwed up his face before he spoke.

"And what do it fuckin' matter?" he shot back. "If a nigga ask you out, all you gotta say is yes or fuckin' no!"

"Well then no!" I snapped right back at him. "Yo' grandma don't like my ass and I ain't riding around with you in her shit! Plus, I date *grown ass men* who have their own house, their own car and their *own* everything else just like I do! I don't want—"

"Oh, but ya ain't worried 'bout all that when you was jumpin' on this dick, was ya?" he asked, embarrassing the fuck out of me when I noticed a few people standing around listening. So then I decided to go for the kill... if he wanted to play this game, I could go there right with him.

"Dick is one thing and a date is another. The bottom line is, I don't fuck with broke niggas because I'm not a broke bitch. If you ain't on my level then you gotta get the hell on!" His jaw clenched as he glared at me but I wasn't done. "Matter of fact, I got a date at eight tonight with a nigga who is worth my time so I couldn't mess with you tonight anyways."

Cree just looked back at me, his eyes calling me all kinds of shit but his mouth didn't utter a word. Wasn't nothing he could say. He lived with his 'Big Mama'... whether he paid the bill for it or not, that's where he stayed. And he drove around town in *her* shit. Uh uh. I wasn't feeling it.

And, honestly, you could call me anything you want and I'll wear it proudly because, at the end of the day, I worked hard for everything that I had and I'd be damned if I linked up with a nigga who couldn't do the same. I had expensive taste and I wasn't asking for a man to pay for a damn thing for me, but he should be able to if I needed it. My daddy was fine, rich and had it going on. I be damned if I started messing with a man who wasn't the same.

Turning around, I stormed away, leaving Cree in the middle of the sidewalk with a pack of females who obviously ain't have shit to do but sit around and watch us. He didn't say anything to stop me, but I heard the chicks around him trying to sweet talk him into paying them some attention. Maybe he could take them bitches out on a date.

***

Humming, I carefully applied my mascara and then stepped back to admire the work I'd done. I was sexy and I knew it. People always had something to say about 'Instagram models'. They put us in a category like we weren't nothing but whores. Well, this 'whore' attended a prestigious university and was damn near at the top of my class. And I used my page to attract attention and gain followers, but I'd managed to turn that into a business by doing paid advertisements and modeling clothes on my page. All that said, I still had a little ratchet in me because that's who I was, but I was on my shit and I'd be damned if I got with someone who wasn't. I knew my worth. And that's why I had denied the date with broke ass Cree to go out with rich ass pretty boy, Donny.

Donny was an investment banker who I'd been talking to online after he hit me up on Facebook. And yeah, he was boring in some ways but, in other ways, he was exactly what I wanted. Meaning: he had his own shit. He was also sexy, reminding me of a young Morris Chestnut who was steadily growing into his finest with age. He was only a few years older than me, but it felt like he was much older because he was so successful and carried himself that way also.

My phone rang just as I was slipping my feet into some nude stiletto heels that matched perfectly with the nude, 'barely there' lace mini dress that I had on. It fit my hips snuggly, showing off my plump backside and tiny waist while also bringing attention to my long, shapely legs. Donny was going to be working overtime to hide an erection as soon as he saw me, and that was just what I wanted.

"Hello?"

"Hey... just making sure that you don't want me to send a car to pick you up." I smiled, listening to Donny ask me once again if I wanted him to send someone to drive me to our date. He was a gentleman and initially wanted to scoop me up from Janelle's place but I politely refused, not wanting to have him take a trip to the hood in order to grab me. I understood Janelle liked to pay for her own things but homegirl was tripping. Our daddy never had us living in the hood growing up, and I'd be damned if I lived there by choice as a grown ass woman.

"No, I'm good, but thank you for asking. I'm just going to meet you there. I'm calling a cab," I told him, still smiling into the phone as I stood and admired my appearance in Janelle's floor-length mirror.

"Okay, baby. Can't wait to see you," he told me sexily.

"I know," I cockily replied and hung up the phone. Now that was how you were supposed to treat a woman. Cree could take some hints.

Checking the time, I grabbed up my gold clutch and walked out of the room. Janelle was seated on the couch with her head stuck in a book. Why was I not surprised? I thought that she had been hitting it off with Cree's brother, Luke—with his sexy ass—but I guess not.

"You heading out?" she asked me, closing the book she was reading and laying it in her lap.

"Yes, I am. With Donny… remember I was telling you about him?"

She nodded her head and I waltzed over to where she was, sitting next to her. I was going to be late meeting up with Donny since I'd only just used the app on my phone to call a cab, but he'd be alright. Beautiful things took time, right?

"Yeah, I remember," she said, unenthused. I could tell there was something else on her mind.

"What are you going to be doing tonight?" I asked her, suddenly concerned about leaving her alone. I was always trying to get Janelle out the house, but she was such a homebody, studying all the damn time. I understood that work was important to her but everybody needed a break.

"I'm just going to stay in, probably go to bed early. Val has been out late since that incident the other day, and I'm just trying to avoid her until I can move out of here," she told me with a sigh.

"I wish I had been here so I could've beat that bitch's ass for you. I haven't ran into her yet but trust, I will before I leave and I got something waiting too." Janelle looked at me like she wanted to say something to stop me, but one look at the seriousness in my eyes and she knew there was no use.

"So you definitely decided to move," I said, changing the subject. "That's good, too, because you too naïve to be living in the hood."

Janelle rolled her eyes and smiled at me. "Oh, and you're not?" she asked.

"I'm not as naïve as you but still… I wouldn't be living here. I need to be able to experience the finer things in life."

Janelle rolled her eyes and I laughed as I got up to leave. Once I stepped outside, I started walking down the stairs and nearly toppled over the last step when I saw the flyest ride I'd ever seen pull up in front of me. It was a cream Maybach with gold rims and dark tinted windows. That shit was sick.

A huge grin came on my face when I looked at it, realizing that Donny thought he was slick. I'd told him over and over again not to send a car for me and this nigga did it anyways. How he got the address… who knows? That was the thing about dating men who were entrepreneurs. They were go-getters. It didn't matter what it was, they had a way of getting the job done.

But when the door opened up and the person in the driver's side stood up, I froze and my mouth dropped open. Your girl was so stunned that a small breeze could have knocked me over! Donny was not who got out of the car. Instead, my eyes landed right on Cree. And he was looking delicious enough to eat.

Standing in front of me with a fresh cut and some nice ass designer jeans with a simple white Polo tee, white Polo vest and some white and gold Giuseppes, Cree was hood rich fine. On his neck, he wore a few simple gold Cuban link chains, and his wrists were iced out in diamond bracelets on one wrist and a banging ass watch on the other. His style was always on point but nobody could mess with him in this moment. He had it all together, rendering me utterly speechless.

"W—what are you doing here?" I asked him when I finally found my voice, as I took a few small steps forward.

"I'm taking you out," he replied with a shrug. He stuffed his hands in his pockets and took a deep breath as he looked at me and I creamed. Cree isn't the youngest, but he had a baby face that made him look a lot younger than Luke, who was the youngest. He acted like a little young spoiled brat sometimes too, which annoyed the shit out of me but, in this moment, he had my ass feeling like I was in love.

"But I'm going out already…" I said, suddenly remembering Donny. "My cab should be here any minute to—"

"So you turned down a date wit' ya boy to go chill wit' a nigga who was gon' have you ridin' in a fuckin' cab?" Cree asked, frowning.

"He wasn't—he asked me if I wanted him to send a car but I—"

"Send a car? So he couldn't pick you up from ya spot?"

"NO!" I groaned, rolling my eyes as I started to get annoyed. "He was but—you know what? You can't even talk! How you gon' come here with this rented car and then try to hate on the next nigga?"

"Rented?" he repeated with a frown. He took a step forward, looking down at me. I sucked in the scent of his cologne and nearly swooned.

"This shit ain't *rented!*" he declared, pointing back at the car. "I bought it… cash. Check the paper tag on the back, ma. You was trippin' and actin' like a nigga ain't have shit, so I pulled one on ya spoiled ass to show you how you was on some bullshit."

"What?" I whispered, peeking at the nice ass ride behind him. Then I looked from the car, back at him and then at the car again.

"Damn," was all I could say. Yes… me, Carmella, the one who could never shut up for a second, even to save my life, had absolutely nothing to say. He'd showed up and showed the fuck out!

"Right… now tell whoever you thought you was goin' out wit' that yo' little date is cancelled," he instructed, giving me a look that dared me to do otherwise.

Damn, I said again, this time in my mind. He was regulating shit, putting me in my place and romanticizing the hell out of me all at the same time. Only Cree could pull some shit like that. Only Cree could diss you, make you feel dumb as hell and flatter you all in one.

"Okay," I told him in a quiet voice, and I saw Cree's expression soften when he saw that he'd won and I'd finally backed down to respect the thug in him. I almost wanted to pick a fight with him just because I saw that he felt like he won something, but I decided not to.

Cree turned around and walked to the passenger side to open the door for me and I was right behind him, not saying a word because there was too much on my mind. Tomorrow, I had to fly back to Cali and here I was making something with Cree that I knew I couldn't finish. That was the real reason I'd shot him down to go out with Donny because, if I were true to myself, I'd admit that I was feeling Cree. What would I do when it was time to leave?

Why Am I In Love With Him?

Sidney

"*Y*ou such a fuckin' bum ass nigga, Tank!" Faviola yelled as I looked on. She snapped her neck and waved her head back and forth when she talked, making her long, platinum blond weave catch me right in the face. Stepping back, I brushed it away and put my game face on. I was standing behind her, ready to jump in if need be even though I knew her ass was dead wrong for what she was doing.

"Man, chill wit' all dat shit! I'on even know why you brought ya ass over here because I told you I ain't doin' shit until I find out if that baby is mine!" Tank bellowed back at her.

We were in front of Tank's house and Faviola was doing her favorite thing in the world these days… making a damn scene. I had told her ass not to come over here but she wasn't having it. She had heard from some other chick she hung with that Tank had another girl over at his house, and she had her mind set on busting up whatever they had going on. Problem was, Faviola wasn't his girlfriend so why the hell did she care? Still, she was my best friend so if we were going on a 'beat that nigga's ass' mission, I was here for it.

"You fuckin' know this is your baby for the simple fact that you the one fucked me raw, nigga!"

"Bitch, you fuck everybody raw! You fucked my brother raw!"

"Which brother?" I caught myself saying before I knew it. Faviola looked at me, a crazy look on her face as if she didn't know what I was talking about.

"Huh?"

"Which brother is he talkin' 'bout?" I repeated, frowning in her face. Faviola had never mentioned being with any of the Murrays other than Tank, even though she was always talking about how sexy Kane was too.

"Girl, this stupid ass nigga don't know what he talkin' 'bout! Fuck ass fake thug!" Faviola shot back, holding her hand up like she was going to slap the shit out of Tank. In an instant, Tank's whole demeanor changed. No longer was he the charming laid-back one that I was used to seeing. He completely transformed right before my eyes.

"Lay a muthafuckin' hand on me and I'll show you how fake I really am," Tank said, his voice low and so intense that I felt a shiver run down my own damn spine. His already low set eyes were narrowed into slits as he glared at her with a look that could melt cement in seconds.

Even though Yolo and I had been close when we were younger, I'd never really dealt with any of his brothers other than Cree and Outlaw. Cree was the one I confided in a little about my secret relationship, but my dealings with Outlaw were minimal because he was always so busy fuckin' everything wearing a skirt and a pair of legs. Tank and Kane were a few years older and though Tank was always chill and cool, I was scared as hell of Kane.

"I'm not leaving 'til you bring that bitch out here!" Faviola continued, as she crossed her arms in front of her chest and gave a look like she meant it. She was better than me because I was ready to go with my tail tucked between my legs. It was bad enough that she was over here questioning a man who wasn't even hers.

"Man, chill… I ain't gon' tell you this shit agai—"

Before Tank could finish his sentence, Faviola ducked down, running straight past him and made a beeline to his front door.

"Oh shit!" I yelled, taking off after her to give her some backup in case whatever chick she had heard was inside tried to lay hands on my girl. Faviola was dead wrong but I wasn't about to have nobody touch her. Especially not with her being pregnant.

"THIS DA BITCH TANK FUCKIN' WIT'?!" I heard her yell to no one in particular just as I got to the door. I could hear Tank yelling from behind me but I pushed through anyways, not worried about what he was saying.

There was no one in the front of the house so I assumed Faviola's yelling had come from down the hall. I turned the corner and started running down just in time to hear what sounded like furniture being moved.

"Bitch!"

Damn it, I thought, pissed.

I was not in the mood for this bullshit. This was why I didn't have many friends. I tended to attract hood types because… well, I grew up in the hood and I was hood my damn self. I didn't get along with people who couldn't understand where I came from. That's why I didn't chill with my neighbor's stuck up ass, even though her sister was cool. But back to my point. Hanging with hood bitches meant dealing with hood situations all the fuckin' time. I'd gotten in plenty fights but ain't none of them been mine. It's always been because I had to jump in for one of my homegirls and help them regulate shit.

But as soon as I walked in the room, I saw there wasn't shit that I needed to do. Faviola had ole girl in a headlock and was bamming the shit out of her face. Whoever the girl was, she didn't stand a chance. She was naked and flailing around with her hands in the air, but every time she looked like she was about to do something, Faviola hit her right in the face and knocked that shit back down.

"WHAT DA FUCK?!" Tank boomed from behind me and I stepped aside to let him enter. "Faviola! Yo, get yo' crazy ass outta here, man!"

I watched as Tank came over and tried to break them apart, but Faviola had a stronghold on the naked chick and wasn't letting go.

"Why you gotta be so fuckin' crazy all the damn time! Let go! You done beat her ass already, damn!"

There was movement behind me and I heard a door open. Glancing down the hall, I locked eyes with Yolo and almost jumped like five feet in the air. He had his own spot. What was he doing here?

"Shit, Sidney, what da hell goin' on out there?" he asked, pulling at something around his waist. That's when I realized he wasn't wearing anything but a towel. Damn. He was so damn sexy. Shit… did I really just say that? Fuck, was I falling for his ass again?

"Faviola is—"

I stopped when I saw someone moving behind him. My eyes settled on the figure of a woman who was standing to the side of him, wrapping a sheet around her naked body. Yolo glanced behind his shoulder, seeing what I was looking at and then his eyes came back to mine.

"Fuck," was all he said, his eyes darting around as if he were trying to find more words to say. But there was no point. I came, I saw and now I was out.

"You good," I said with a shrug, putting on the face that I'd perfected over the years of being in love with someone who didn't think I was good enough. Didn't think I was woman enough for him.

"Naw, Sidney, wait…" he said, holding up one finger before ducking in the room and closing the door.

Turning, I looked into Tank's room and saw that he was talking to Faviola, who had her arms crossed in front of her chest as the other girl walked around, picking her clothes up from the floor.

"You gotta chill," he was telling her. "This why I can't deal wit'cha ass on dat level 'cuz you got too much fuckin' attitude!"

Faviola maintained her frown as she stood there with full attitude, tapping one foot against the floor restlessly. Then Tank grabbed her by each of her shoulders and pulled her to him, kissing her right on the lips while the other girl continued picking up her things.

What in the hell is goin' on here?

"Excuse me," the other girl said to me as she pushed by and stormed out the room, leaving Faviola and Tank alone.

"Naw, I'm leavin' too," I muttered as I walked away. I couldn't believe this shit! So Faviola had me come over here on a 'beat that nigga's ass mission' for nothing because, from the looks of it, he was fresh from fuckin' some other bitch and her hoe-ass was about to fuck his ass too. Ain't that some shit. I always knew that out of them all, Tank was the smoothest with the most game because he had more damn kids than I could count. But shit... this nigga was operating on a whole 'nother level.

"Favi, I'll hook up with you later," I yelled, chucking the deuces. She gave me a 'mmhm' in return but didn't even turn in my direction so I bounced.

Just as I got to the front door, I heard footsteps running behind me and I already knew who it was. But I was not Faviola and he was not Tank. Yolo was not about to talk me down after I caught him fuckin' with the next bitch. I was better than that and I was worth so much more.

"Sidney!"

"Naw, nigga," I replied, picking up my pace as I just about ran to my car. He beat me to it and slid his ass right in front of the door, blocking me from opening it.

"Stop," he said, throwing his hands in the air. It was cold outside but he wasn't wearing anything but a hoodie and some basketball shorts with a skully on his head. Still, he looked so effortlessly fine. He licked his lips as he prepared to say his next words and I felt my heart flutter. Why did he have this effect on me? I swear I hated it!

"Whatever you 'bout to say, Yolo, I don't wanna hear it! You don't owe me shit because we not together and never will be. I know you fuck around and you can. You don't have to explain shit to me!" I told him, even though I wished every word I was saying was not true.

"But listen," he started, and I knew it was about to be some bullshit. Every time a nigga got ready to tell you some bullshit, it started with him saying 'But listen'.

"I don't want it to be that way. You know you are my one…" He paused and I felt my resolve turn to mush.

When we were younger, he explained to me what real love was even though I felt like I'd already experienced it with him. He said that there was only one love that was more powerful than any other and that people only experienced it one time in life. He said that kind of love was the love he only had for me and, from then on, he called me his one.

"Just… I wanna talk to you but I can't now," he said and his eyes darted back to the house behind him, reminding me that the reason he couldn't was because of the woman he had in the room. "I just wanna get shit right with you. Can we meet up somewhere tonight? I gotta do some shit at the club wit' my fam but we can meet up after."

My chest began to burn when I listened to what he was saying. Once again, he neglected to invite me to hang with him at the club and suggested that we meet up after. Why couldn't I be with him at the club? Why was I always pushed to later on so he could meet up with me in private when no one was around?

"No thanks," I told him, shaking my head. "Now move."

"Sidney, I—"

"MOVE!" I screamed, pushing him forcefully away. I was sick of his shit and officially done with his ass.

"Alright...damn," he said and he threw his hands in the air, backing away slowly.

I glanced at his face and the hurt in his eyes nearly made my knees buckle, so I avoided his stare and jumped in the car to leave. I couldn't take this shit anymore with Yolo. It was like every time I thought I was able to get over him, something came around and pulled me right back into him.

The love I had for him was consuming to the point that I didn't want it anymore, but I couldn't let him go. Do you understand what it meant to be hopelessly in love? Do you know what it is to love someone so badly that you hate yourself for it? That's where I was and I didn't know how in the world I could change.

Why They Call Him Outlaw.

Janelle

"What you doin'?" Luke asked me, his sexy voice going through my ears and soothing my entire body.

This was crazy, right? And if anybody had ever told me it would happen, I would call their ass a liar. But there was something about Luke that had me feeling a way that I loved and hated at the same time, and the more we talked, the worse it got.

Smiling into the phone, I rolled my eyes as I stood up to walk out my room door.

"Is that any way to greet somebody as soon as they pick up the phone?" I asked him as I opened the door. I groaned inwardly when I heard someone fumbling around with something in the kitchen. It had to be Val because Carmella was out once again. She didn't even live here and had a better social life than me.

"My bad... What yo' fine ass doing?" he asked and I giggled. Yes, I *giggled*. Had I been another woman listening to me, I would have thought it was disgusting.

"Nothing. I was working and listening to some music."

"Music? What kinda music you listen to? Bon Jovi or some shit?"

he asked, and I laughed again.

"No, but what do *you* know about Bon Jo—"

The words completely faded from my mind when I turned the corner into the kitchen and came eye-to-eye with Brandon. Now what the *hell* was he doing here? I couldn't believe that Val was not only still messing with him but that she'd actually invited him back over after what happened the last time he was here.

"You there?" Luke asked, but I couldn't even respond because my eyes were fixed on Brandon who was standing in front of me, wearing nothing but boxers and a wife beater, with a blunt sitting on top of his ear as he drank up *my* orange juice straight from the bottle.

"Sup?" Brandon asked and I immediately hung up the phone on Luke, hoping that he hadn't heard him speak.

Pushing by Brandon, I walked into the kitchen, grabbed something to drink from the fridge, and began searching on the counter for some cookies I'd baked earlier that day. My phone rang again and it was Luke. I shot him a text telling him I would call him back later.

"Oh you lookin' for dem cookies?" Brandon asked, and I almost flinched at the way that his voice made me sick to his stomach.

This was it. I was done trying to do shit on my own from now on. Tomorrow, I would be calling my father and asking him to loan me some money to get the fuck out of here. I could not deal with Val and her creep squad of thug nasties standing around in their disgusting, dingy boxers anymore.

"Yes, where are they?" I let out, finally able to get my mouth to work.

When Brandon didn't answer right away, I turned around to look at him, my eyes narrowing in on the goofy smile on his face. He wasn't ugly. He had a nice fade with an expert lineup, brown skin, and wide doe-like eyes that women usually appreciated on a man. He was somewhat skinny for my taste but had a decent muscle tone to him, so I guess he was alright.

But there was something about him that seemed… slimy. Like he was always up to no good. Maybe it was because I saw him as weak after he'd allowed Luke to punk him in the club. And it didn't help that I knew he'd let someone rape his own sister and didn't do shit about it. I was a good girl at heart, but if anyone tried anything with my sisters, I was ready to go.

"I ate 'em. They was good too," he said, with that smile still pinned to his face like I was supposed to jump and clap my hands at him stating the cookies I'd made for myself were good now that he'd ate them all. Ugh!

Sucking my teeth, I whirled around on my heels and stomped off towards my room, running right into Val as she stepped out of hers. This was the first time I'd seen her since the last incident concerning Brandon but, from the look on her face, she was still feeling the same way she had then.

"He's not leaving. This is as much my place as it is yours," she told me with a frown, and I rolled my eyes. I really was not in the mood to get into it with her today.

One more day, I thought. *One more day and I will be out this shit for good.*

"I'm not trying to fight with you. Do whatever you want, just stay out of my way," I grumbled and walked straight to my room, knocking her with my shoulder in the process.

She was a bitch and if I were honest with myself, I knew that she was never a friend or anyone I should have been rooming with. We were too different and, even though I tried to help her, it didn't matter. Some people couldn't be helped.

Somewhere in between reading and listening to music on my headphones to block out the sound of Val's moans of pleasure, I feel asleep and I awoke hours later to the sound of my phone ringing in my ear.

"Hello?" I grumbled into the phone, not even thinking to see who it was calling me first. I just needed to stop that damn ringing.

"Yo, what da fuck is all that noise comin' from ya crib?" Luke asked, but I could barely hear him.

Pressing my finger to my ear, I squinted as I tried to make out what he was saying through all the music around me. Wait… music?! Who the hell was blasting rap songs at this time of the morning?

"Uh… I don't know," I said honestly, as I stood up and grabbed my robe from around the chair in my room. It sounded like Val was playing music for the whole damn neighborhood. Turning around, I glanced at the clock on my dresser. It was 4:08 in the morning! What the hell was she doing?

"You don't know? I just drove by that shit and saw niggas posted outside and shit. Then you hung up on me earlier and I know I heard a nigga talkin'. You gon' make me spazz da fuck out if—"

"Hold on," I cut in, dropping the phone on the bed as I pushed my feet into my slippers.

Unlocking my door, I opened it and was greeted with a face full of smoke. Weed. Although I'd never smoked it before, I knew the smell. Carmella smoked weed *all* the time when we were younger, and was always enlisting me to help her cover the scent.

As soon as my eyes adjusted to the smoke and the dim lighting, I saw that the entire apartment was covered with people, mostly men and a few women. All of them eating, drinking, dancing, or damn near fuckin' wherever there was space, whether it be in the living room, kitchen or dining room.

"What the hell…" I gasped as I walked out cautiously, slowly placing one foot ahead of the other as I looked around. Then my eyes fell on someone sitting on the couch with *my* laptop on *his* legs, using it like it was his own. How he managed to get by my passcode, I had no idea. Running over, I snatched it from him and tucked it under my arm. I was pissed off to the max.

"This is *mine!*" I screamed at him as he shrugged, smiling like I was joking around. "Don't touch my shit!"

"This is *mine!*" Brandon mocked me and I turned around, scowling at him.

He was sitting on the loveseat with Val tucked under his arms. Only she didn't look like herself at all. I was used to her barely being dressed so that wasn't abnormal. But her eyes were glassy and unfocused. She was drunk and she was high, I could tell. But whatever she was on looked like it was much more than just some weed.

"Val, I work for the—" I paused, not wanting everyone to know my business. "You *know* you can't do this in here. You'll get me fired!"

"You'll get me fired!" Brandon parroted again as Val laughed hard like it was the funniest joke in the world. He was so fuckin' lame it was sickening. Then he stood up in front of me and I glared at him, clutching my laptop in front of my chest to create a barrier between us.

"You need to loosen up, ma," he said and pulled at the strings of my robe, making it come open and reveal the bra and panties I was wearing underneath. He and everyone around, including Val, laughed as I struggled to hold the laptop and get my robe closed. I felt my cheeks twinge with shame when I finally got it closed.

"You're such a fuckin' dumb ass," I spat, clutching my robe as I started to walk by. But Brandon wasn't done trying to embarrass me. Reaching out, he ripped the laptop from my hands and snatched at my robe again.

"And you a bitch," he shot back, his facial expression shifting to a cold serious look that let me know he was just getting started with me. Grabbing my arm, he pulled me forcefully forward.

"You just think your pussy is special because you fuckin' wit' Outlaw, huh?" he asked, a malicious smirk on his lips. "I'on give a fuck 'bout dat nigga and you can tell him I said it."

"Yeah, and newsflash, bitch. Outlaw fucks wit' everyone," a chick said, and everyone in the room began to laugh, mumbling in agreement.

I started to struggle against Brandon but he only held me tighter, laughing at me the more I struggled. Then I started to panic when I felt hands on my body. I turned around to see who it was, but somebody started playing with the lights, switching them on and off so that my eyes couldn't focus. There was more laughter and I felt my breathing speed up as I started to spazz out.

"Yo, fam, you need to stop," a male voice laughed. "You scaring that bitch!"

More laughter. More hands. I started to fight back with my one hand, punching at everything I could, including Brandon, who was still holding me firmly in his grasp.

"What, you don't wanna have a little fun?" he asked. He managed to grab my other hand and I screamed when I felt him pull me close to his body. I could feel his hard dick against my ass and he began to grind it hard into me. Bile began to tickle the back of my throat and I gagged, feeling like I was going to throw up.

"Yo, kill the switch," Brandon instructed and, instantly, the room went black, except for a single black light that came on, showing me why most of the people in the room were wearing white. Their shirts glowed and I screamed again when I saw men surrounding me, unable to see any of their faces.

"LET ME GO!"

"What, you scared? No need to be scared. Just chill, ma," another man said, and Brandon laughed as he rubbed his erection against the crack of my ass.

"Val! Please!" I screamed, tears stinging my eyes just as I felt another pair of hands pulling at my panties. Another hand pushed up under my bra, fiddling with my breasts. Brandon leaned down and kissed me on my neck, sucking hard on my skin until it began to burn.

"LET ME GO!" I screamed once more, this time thrashing about wildly with my elbows, pulling and stomping whatever I could.

"SHIT!" Brandon yelled when I stomped hard on his foot. He loosened his grip on my arm and that was all I needed. I took off down the hall to my room, slamming the door behind me.

"Leave dat borin' bitch alone. Almost jammed my fuckin' toe!" I heard Brandon say on the other side of the door.

I was breathing so hard that it felt like my lungs were on fire and my heart felt like it was going to beat through my chest. Grabbing my phone, I didn't even think to dial 9-1-1. I needed to speak to Luke. Seeing that he'd hung up, I called him back and he answered on the first ring just as someone started banging on the door.

"Open up and let me taste that sweet pussy!" the voice said and I cringe, glancing around for somewhere to hide. Then I heard Luke's voice.

"Yo, I'm tired of you hangin' up the fuckin' phone in my—"

"Luke!" I was able to get out through my tears. "I—I—"

I stopped when I heard more heavy banging on my door, so hard that it seemed like it would burst from the hinges. A loud sob escaped my lips and I squeezed my eyes closed.

"What is all that fuckin' noise? And… is you cryin'?" he asked and it only made me wail even harder.

Biting my lip, I tried to will myself to stop so I could tell Luke everything that happened. I blurted it all out as fast as I could, hoping that he could understand. But when I was done, the line went silent. Pulling the phone away, I stared at it, wondering if the call had dropped.

"Hello?"

"Aye, where you at now?" he asked, his voice low, flat and void of his normal joking tone that I was used to hearing. It sent chills through me and my heart skipped a beat.

"In my room."

"Stay there. No matter what you hear, stay there," was all he said and then he hung up.

Dropping the phone, I scooted to the top of my bed and curled up with my arms around my raised legs and my back planted against the headboard. The knocking had finally stopped but I still wasn't at ease. I stayed there for I didn't know how long, listening to the thumping of the music and the sounds of laughter outside my door as Luke's words cycled through my mind.

Stay there. No matter what you hear, stay there.

My breathing had finally returned to normal, when I heard a loud noise coming from what I assumed was the front door. It was so loud that even my walls rattled. Instantly, I panicked and grabbed my legs tighter in my arms, caging myself in. Until I heard his voice.

"GET ON DA FUCKIN' GROUND NOW!"

Luke was here. His words were followed by screaming and a lot of scurrying as people moved around. Then my heart was nearly ripped from my chest when I heard the loud wailing of a man. I couldn't even make out who it was screaming. All I could think was that it might have been Luke. I instantly forgot about how scared I was only seconds before, and got up, bolting out of my room door.

But it wasn't Luke at all.

As soon as I got down the hall, I saw that everyone who had been laughing at me earlier was on the floor, bellies down with their hands in the air. The only ones standing were Luke and his brothers, all of them, except the one I'd seen Carmella talking to that one night at the club.

Seeing me dash from down the hall, all of their eyes came up on me, everyone of them but Luke raising their arms and pointing weapons in my direction. Screaming, I stopped short, throwing my hands in the air and diving to the ground, plopping down right on my ass. After noticing it was me, they dropped their weapons and my eyes flew over to Luke who was still staring at me. But I knew then that Luke wasn't who I was staring at. I was looking at Outlaw for the very first time.

His eyes were pulled tight, delivering a glare so vicious that even I had to cower from it and look away. It seemed like he didn't even recognize me… like he was someone totally different from the man I'd come to know. I was scared shitless. I'd never seen him this way and the only thing I could do was thank God that I wasn't his enemy.

His brothers stood around him with the same threatening glares in their eyes. Even the one they called Yolo, who seemed to be the life of the party that one night at the club. These were the gangsters that Pelmington was trying to put away. These were the Murray brothers.

I snatched my head up when I heard a loud noise followed by

an excruciating scream from the same man who I'd heard earlier and thought was Luke. It was Brandon. He was on the ground, lying with his belly down but his face was bloody and his nose was busted, as if he'd gotten kicked in the face a few times.

"Leave him alone, please!" Val screamed but everyone ignored her.

"Pick his ass up," one of Luke's brothers said. I assumed he was the oldest one from how the others immediately began to do as he asked.

"Play time over. We gotta get da fuck outta here."

"NO!" Val yelled and I watched as she ran over, fists raised as she began hitting on Luke as he grabbed at Brandon's arms.

Luke swirled around with lightning fast speed, knocking her back forcefully with the side of his arm and making her fall onto the floor. She started moving forward like she was about to try to run at him again, but he pulled out a gun, shooting her an icy glare as he shook his head no. My eyes were wide as I watched on, scared to the point that my knees were knocking. Who was this man?

I cradled my legs with my arm, falling into a position that provided me the most comfort when I felt like I needed it. I watched with wide eyes as two of Luke's brothers pulled Brandon out of the living room and through the front door, as he howled in protest while the older brother watched on to make sure they did as he instructed. I felt a heated stare on me and that's when I finally lifted my head to look at Luke, almost debating against it for fear of what I'd see. The steel look in his eyes remained, but there was a calmness behind them that told me I had no reason to be afraid of him. Still, I was.

He walked over to me and held out a hand, like he was going to touch my hair. I flinched. I didn't mean to but I did anyways. I was scared out of my mind and it was a wonder that the only thing I'd done was flinch and not peed on my damn self.

Luke pulled back and he held my stare for a minute. I watched as the flame in his eyes died down and the caring look I enjoyed to see, finally began to shine through.

"No need to be afraid of me, ma," he said finally. "But I told you to stay in the room. I said, 'no matter what you hear, stay there'. Let this be the last time you don't listen. Let this be the last time you don't trust me."

He locked my eyes into his for a few seconds longer, making sure that his words sunk through before sighing and turning away.

"Everybody else, get da fuck outta here," he said, kicking at the leg of one of the guys on the floor nearby. "And you know what da fuckin' deal is. You ain't see shit because ain't shit happen."

And with that, I watched as everyone began to get up and run towards the door, eager to be let free. Luke walked over and looked at Val, just before he walked out the door.

"Get ya ass up and clean all this shit up," he said to her and her eyes shot wide open.

"But I—"

She stopped and I could only guess that Luke had given her a look to stop her right in the middle of her protest. Her shoulders dropped and she got up, shooting me a piercing glance right before she began picking up a cup on the floor next to where she sat. Luke watched her as she placed it into the trashcan. Then he kicked another cup toward her that was full of alcohol, watching the liquid splash against her legs before walking to the door.

"I'll holla at ya later, Janelle," was the last thing he said before he left, leaving me and Val alone.

I sat in that place, frozen for a few seconds after he disappeared. I couldn't move because I was trying to process everything that had just occurred in the last hour. It wasn't until I heard the shrill screams of Brandon outside, that I was awakened from my trance. Val ran into the kitchen and ripped the blinds apart, staring outside to see what was going on as I heard the sound of car engines starting.

"OH MY GOD!" she cried, placing her hand over her mouth. "They have him tied up to the back of a car. They are going to drag him down the fuckin'—oh my God!"

The sound of the engines increased and I clamped my hand over my ears as Val screamed loudly, tears running down her face. Then she whirled around, her hand out as she pointed accusingly at me.

"THIS IS ALL YOUR FAULT! THIS IS ALL YOUR FUCKIN' FAULT!"

She ran up on me with her fists raised as if she was about to hit me and I braced myself, scrambling to my feet so that I could even out the battlefield. But then she stopped suddenly, falling into a fit of tears, crying agonizingly, as she dropped her face into her hands.

Staring, I didn't move a muscle to console her. The image of her laughing as Brandon and his friends humiliated me was still vivid in my mind, and I couldn't bring myself to feel sorry for her or him either.

The Janelle from before would have been horrified at the thought of what I'd just seen happen in front of my face, but I wasn't the least bit regretful for any of it.

For the first time, I was starting to understand why Luke and his brothers did some of the things they were accused of. Brandon's own sister had been raped and he would have done the same to me, had he been given the chance. For some people, the law I believed in just wasn't severe enough and they needed another form of punishment. And for them, there was Luke. I guess that's why they called him Outlaw.

"Clean all this up, like he said, and then pack up your shit and get out. You're no longer welcome here," I told Val before turning around and walking down the hall to my room.

She was still standing at the entrance of the hall looking at me when I slammed the door in her face, but I knew she would do as I said. She'd seen what Luke was capable of so I was positive I wouldn't have to worry about her ever again.

Fans.

Carmella

I was having the time of my life! Cree probably couldn't say the same thing, but it wasn't my fault that he couldn't take being on a date with a woman *this* fine. He must've been used to only fuckin' with ugly ass chicks but that was not me!

"Hey, can I take a pic with you?" a guy asked as he walked up to me. He was cute in a nerdy kind of way, nice brown skin, cute fade and neat clothing. Too neat. He was obviously gay.

"Baby girl, I've been following you on Instagram for years and I can't believe that I actually ran into you," he continued to gush as Cree stood by my side, looking like he wanted to punch the shit out of him. The guy was so focused on me, he didn't even notice Cree by my side. That's probably what was pissing him off.

"Of course, hunny!" I told him, smiling brightly. "Just make sure to tag my page when you post it!"

"I will!" he agreed excitedly. Then for the first time since he walked over, he turned to Cree. "Can you take the picture, bro?"

"I'm not your fuckin' br—"

"Cree! Please, can you just take it? Damn!" I barked at him, annoyed that he was being such a baby.

The nightclub that Cree took me to was in downtown Manhattan, and it was live. The first thirty minutes that we were there, he and I had been having a good ass time, drinking, dancing and actually talking without arguing. Then I posted where I was on my Instagram page and shit took a turn for the worse. A few of my followers were in the club and started coming over for my pictures and to talk, and some who weren't in the club and saw the message decided to stop by to meet me. Instead of relishing in the attention like I did, Cree started to have a bitch fit and that brings us here.

"This the last fuckin' pic I'm takin', Mel," he said, snatching the phone from the guy and giving him a dirty look before standing up. I rolled my eyes and tried to keep myself from cursing his ass out.

Standing up, I half-turned to the camera, doing my signature pose that showed off my ass. The guy came around and wrapped one arm around me, posing with me as we both smiled at the camera. Cree half ass took the picture and was about to hand over the phone, when the guy told him to wait.

"I need another pic. Like a goofy one. Let's boot our asses at the camera!" he yelled and I screamed, laughing excitedly with him.

"Let's go for it!" Turning, we both booted to the camera and turned to look at it with duck faces as we waited for Cree to take the pic.

"Hell to the *fuck* no!" Cree yelled, tossing the camera on the bar table before stomping off.

"CREE!" I yelled out but he didn't turn around. Turning back to the man by my side, I began to apologize profusely.

"I'm so sorry… he's not used to all this," I told him.

The man smacked his lips and snapped his neck as he looked at me like he knew exactly what I was talking about.

"Baby girl, it will take a special kind of man to understand all the fierceness that is you," he said with a three-point snap and I laughed. "I mean, I love you but I can't hang 'round a bitch like you either. You'd steal all my thunder!"

Laughing, I leaned over and hugged him, then took his number down before going to find Cree. I really couldn't believe how he was acting. Yes, he might have thought being an Instagram model wasn't shit but it was how I was able to afford things for myself. I wasn't balling out of control off of it but it stopped me from having to ask my daddy for everything.

"What is your problem?!" I yelled when I found Cree sitting outside on the corner, smoking a blunt. He was right out in the open like he didn't give a damn that what he was doing was illegal. What kind of man was this that I was with?

"I ain't wit' dat shit, Mel," he said, blowing out the smoke. "I came here to chill wit' you, not be ya fuckin' paparazzi."

Folding my arms in front of my chest, I glared at him as he shot a stare of his own right back at me.

"It's not my fault! I didn't ask for them to come! But when my fans want pics, I give it to them because I'm trying to make a career out of this. I—"

"You tryin' to make a fuckin' career out of showing your ass on Instagram?!" he snapped, standing up so quickly that he nearly bumped into me. A few people around us shot us looks as they passed by, curious about what was going on, although they didn't want to stop and stare.

"I don't show my ass on—"

"Yes you fuckin' do!" Reaching down, he held up his phone screen and I saw that he'd been scrolling through my page. "Most of ya fuckin' pics on here are of you in lingerie or some shit that barely covers ya damn ass. You're smart as hell but I can't tell that shit from ya fuckin' page! You think I'm cool wit' niggas approachin' my girl for pics just because they like to see her twerking her ass for the Gram?"

"*Your* girl?" I snapped back at him, batting his phone from my face. "First off, I'm *not* your girl. Secondly, I'm a grown ass woman which means I can do whatever the fuck I want to do. Thirdly, I get paid for what I'm doing which is much better than living off a man who thinks he can tell me what to do with my life. I got a bangin' body and maybe ten more years left of showing it to whoever I fuckin' please before I decide to settle down and have kids. And if I wanna do that shit, I'mma do it!"

"Well, do it, baby!" somebody said, but neither one of us moved as we stared at each other. Both of us were stubborn as hell and we couldn't have it any other way than our way. There was no way that this would work and I was finally seeing that. But it was a good thing. It wasn't like I stayed in New York. We were doomed to be a one-night stand from the beginning. The one night just lasted way too long.

"You know what? Just take me the fuck home. I leave for Cali tomorrow morning so, after tonight, we'll be done with this shit anyways and you won't have to worry about me anymore," I spat at him, feeling near tears. But I be damned if I cry because of this nigga. Cree wasn't shit. I'd been through many breakups before and I never cried over them, so I be damned if I do it for someone I'd only known for about a week.

"Wait," Cree started, his eyes narrowing at me. "You're flying back to Cali?"

"Yes. Tomorrow," I repeated, trying to hold my face straight.

See, although I had told Cree that I was coming in to visit Janelle, I'd never told him when I was leaving. I guess he assumed that I would be staying a lot longer than I was. Well, you know what they say about when you assume something. And he'd made an ass out of himself in many ways already as far as I was concerned.

"And when were you gonna tell me that shit, Mel?" he asked. I noticed that the way he was looking at me had changed. It was almost like he was more hurt than angry.

"Why does it matter? You knew I was leaving! I don't live here. What we had was always going to end anyways," I stopped, the reality of my words creating a pang in my chest the more I spoke. I had to go.

"You know what? Can you just take me back? I don't wanna be here anymore," I told him, biting my bottom lip. His eyes lowered to my lips before coming back up and then he nodded his head.

"C'mon," was the last thing he said to me all night.

***

I woke up early the next morning and began packing my things, only pausing to tell Janelle bye. She had briefly filled me in on what happened the night before but I knew she was skipping out on some details so I didn't feel bad for not being there for her. That made me feel like shit but I was glad Cree's brothers had been able to help her.

I would miss my sister. Out of all of us, Janelle and I were the closest. Not to say that we weren't all close, because we were. It was just that Janelle was my best friend. Part of me wished that I could extend the trip because I hadn't spent much time with her, but I couldn't. My vacation was over and I had exams coming up before Thanksgiving break.

"Be careful," Janelle told me as I rolled my eyes through the phone.

"I will, Jani! Don't you have work to do? This is like your tenth time calling me this morning!" I said as I zipped up my duffle bag.

"Yes, but… I just wish you had stayed longer. Especially with Val gone now. I guess I'll miss you," she said. I got the feeling that there was something that she wanted to tell me from her tone and, even though I need to get my ass out the house, I took the bait.

"What's wrong?" She paused but I knew she wanted to talk so I just waited.

"Well… you know Cree's brother? Luke?" she started and I tried to ignore the sadness that washed over me when she mentioned Cree.

"Yes, the fine ass one. Looks kinda crazy… wild eyes?" I asked, pulling an image of him up in my mind.

"Yes," Janelle chuckled a little. "Him. He… he spent the night a couple nights back. He didn't leave until the morning."

"Oh, *that's* why your ass had the door locked and put covers and shit on the couch for me?" I retorted as I ran through everything that had happened on the day she was referring to. I figured that Janelle had been in one of her moods and wanted time alone. But turns out, she had a man in there.

"Isn't he a little… different from your normal type?" I asked, frowning into the phone with a little smile on my face. I couldn't help but be intrigued. This was not the Janelle I knew. I almost laughed when she sighed deeply before answering.

"Yes," was all she said but I could read so much more behind that statement.

"But you like him anyways?"

"Yes," she said again, but I could hear the emotion in her tone. No, she was doing more than liking his ass. She loved him and she may not have picked up on it yet but I had.

"Well, do what makes you happy," I told her and then tried to ignore the sting in my chest. I was giving her advice that I needed to be giving my damn self when it came to Cree. Well, maybe not. Cree made me happy only sometimes. The other times, his ass made me mad as hell.

"But what about daddy and—"

"Jani, you always worried about the wrong things! Live your life and let other people live theirs. Who cares what daddy thinks?!" I shot back at her. I was annoyed that I had to tell her the same exact thing that I'd said so many times before.

Now that was some true shit. Janelle was always the one out of all of us who was so consumed with what daddy wanted that she ignored what she wanted. I wasn't cursed with that shit. I did my own thing and I didn't give a damn about what anyone thought. Now, I loved and respected my daddy but I knew that his ass wasn't going anywhere! He wouldn't disown me so I was going to live my life.

"Would you introduce Daddy to Cree?" she asked, and I stopped for a second to think of it. Truthfully, I didn't know. I'd never introduced daddy to any of the men I dealt with, simply because they never stuck around long enough.

"If it got to that, I would. But Cree and I aren't there yet," I said, honestly.

"You do know that Cree is a Murray, right?"

"Yes, that's his last name… I know that," I said, even though what I really wanted to say was "DUH!". I had no issues sleeping around but I wasn't that bad… I at least got a nigga's last name before I let him get it.

"No, he's a Murray brother. I made a copy of some papers from a case I was working on. It's on my desk. Read them and you'll see what I mean," she told me and I frowned, wondering what in the world she was hinting at.

"Okay… well, I have to go. I'll call you when I board the plane."

After reassuring her a million times that I would be safe, I finally hung up, called a cab, and grabbed my bags to walk out. Before walking down the stairs, I set something on Sidney's doorstep; a parting gift that I knew she would thank me for later.

The app on my phone told me that the cab would take about ten minutes, but I was ready to go and sick of sitting in the apartment alone. Also… a small part of me was hoping that I'd walk out and see Cree, walking down the street with those damn headphones in his ears. I really didn't want to leave without seeing him but my pride wouldn't let me call his ass first.

But when I walked down the steps, I got the shock of my life. There was a cab parked out front waiting on me but that wasn't the surprise, even though I had only just called it. Standing outside the cab was Cree, and he was holding a McDonald's bag in one hand, a coffee cup in the other, and a lopsided grin on his handsome face.

"What are you doin' here?!" I asked him as I strode forward, biting back the smile that was coming to my face.

"Waiting on you. I remember how hard it was for you to get a cab before, so I figured I'd bring one to you," he said with a shrug. He handed me the bag and the coffee in exchange for my duffle bag.

"It's cold," I noted, taking a sip of the coffee.

"You don't know how long I been standin' my ass out here, waiting for you to come out. If ya ass was ever on time, it would've been hot," he muttered as he tossed my stuff in the back of the cab. I was impressed. Cree might not always do or say the right things, but he was thoughtful when it counts… well, sometimes.

"Let's go," he said and I nodded my head, sliding into the passenger side when he held the door open for me.

I felt butterflies fluttering around in my stomach, like I was a little girl. He made me feel like a girl and a woman all at the same time. One second we would be fighting like elementary students, and the next second he'd do something like this, reminding me that he was a grown man in every way. What the hell was I going to do with him?

I watched as Cree walked to the other side and that's when I remembered the papers in my hand that I'd grabbed from Janelle's desk. I folded them and stuffed them in my purse just as he got into the driver's side.

"You ready?" he asked, looking at me.

No.

"Yes," I said and looked away, finally checking out the inside of the car. It was an actual cab... like had all the actual equipment inside.

"How did you get this?" I asked, frowning as I continued to look at everything. Cree paused and I brought my eyes to him and the apprehensive look on his face.

"Uh... You don't want to know," was all he said. I shot him a curious glance but dropped the subject. Everything about this cab situation was screaming 'illegal'.

We rode to the airport in silence as I admired the scenery outside. I couldn't help it. I loved everything about New York. It was so different from Cali in so many ways but I loved it all. Somewhere along the way, Cree grabbed my hand and placed it on his lap. I tried to keep my cool about it, but a sexual volcano erupted inside of me from having my hand so close to the anaconda trapped inside of his pants. God, if he would have asked me right then to stay, I probably would have.

"We're here," he said, as if he really had to announce it once we made it to JFK. Pulling up curbside, I took a deep breath as I unlaced my fingers from his and reached down to grab my purse. Cree got out of the car and grabbed my things from the back as I let myself out.

Coming to my side, he stood in front of me and there was an awkward silence as we looked at each other. Neither one of us knew what to say.

"I'll see you around," Cree said finally as he shoved my bag at me. My mouth dropped open when I saw him turn to head back to the cab. Like really, nigga?!

"You did *all* of this to just say that?!" I snapped at his back as he walked away. He stopped suddenly and swiveled around, the intensity that I was used to seeing, lingering in his eyes.

Glaring at me, he said, "What?!"

I dropped the duffle bag from my hands and stepped up close to him, ready to go off. No one but Cree could take me from zero to muthafuckin' a million this damn fast.

"The cab, this stale ass breakfast, driving me here… you did all this to just say 'see you around' and that's it?!"

"Fuck! What da hell do you want from a nigga, Mel? Everything I do, you're never fuckin' satisfied! Ain't it obvious I'm feelin' you? But you're still leavin' so what da fuck do you expect me to say?!"

Hell, I had no idea what I expected him to say but, damn, can a bitch get a kiss on the lips or something bef ⌐lane to go across the country? He was acting like I wasr damn near every day since I'd been here. I this nigga how to act!

"Forget it," I muttered, reaching dov expect shit from you except exactly wha Cree."

And with that, I turned on my heels and started walking briskly away as tears came to my eyes. Tears! Can you believe this shit?

"Mel, I—" he started but then stopped short. Exhaling, I turned around and saw that he was looking at a man who was reaching for the handle on the back door of the cab.

"Get da fuck back, nigga! Do I look like a fuckin' taxi driver to you?" Cree barked, making the man damn near jump three feet in the air. Confused, the man looked from Cree to the cab and then back to Cree before muddling away.

Then Cree looked up, locking me in his gaze and I could see that he was pleading silently for me to get in the car and stay. And do what though? Leave behind my whole life in Cali to chill with him in the hood? Then my mind went to the papers that I'd stuffed in my purse. I hadn't even had a chance to read them. I still needed to know what he was all about.

"Mel, c'mon, man," he started, sounding like he was struggling with his words. "You want me to tell you not to leave? Okay, then don't leave. Get back in the car… Is that what you want me to say? Don't go."

I was torn between body and mind. My mind was telling me to get back in the car with Cree and figure shit out another day while wrapped up in his arms. But my feet wouldn't move. To be honest, it had only been a week. As much as I felt for him, I didn't even know that I'd be signing up for if I decided to be with him. But Cree didn't for me to decide. He took my hesitancy as a no.

it then," he grumbled, waving me off with one hand, and I ash to a million pieces inside my chest.

He turned around and jumped in the driver's side of his ride. I watched as he gave life to the engine, before recklessly pulling out in front of another car and tearing down the road. My eyes pinned on the last place he'd been before he disappeared around the corner. I realized I was devastated but, more than anything, I was confused.

It had only been a week. *One* damn week. Why did I feel like I was losing the man that I loved?

That Type of Girl.
Sidney

"Shit! Bitch, who the fuck am I lookin' at right now?!" Faviola asked as she circled around me, eyeing me up and down as if she couldn't believe her eyes.

I didn't blame her. I couldn't believe mine either, to be honest. Carmella had left me with a gift that I wasn't sure I wanted at first. But after looking at it and texting her back and forth for a while, I decided to try something new. In a bag by my door, she'd left a few dresses, some makeup that I didn't know what the hell to do with, a flat iron, some heels and a few other things.

I tried everything on and it fit perfectly, surprising even myself with the way I looked. Then I FaceTimed her and she walked me through how to apply the makeup and flat iron my hair. After hours of work, I loved the result. I didn't even know my hair had a lil' bit of length to it because I always kept it up in a ponytail so I could keep it out the way. But now that I actually had done something with it, I saw it was damn near to my bra line. Now, was I going to do this shit every day? Hell naw! But it would work tonight in order to prove a point.

"You like it?" I asked Faviola and she stepped back, placing her hand at her chest like she couldn't believe I'd even asked.

"Hell yeah, I *love* it. Who gave you some dick and knocked the tomboy out of you?" she asked and I laughed, sitting down on the bed with my legs gaped open just like I was one of the boys.

"Bitch, ain't nobody take shit out of me. I just figured I'd swap up my style before we go out tonight," I shrugged, but she gave me a knowing look.

"Aw, naw. I know what you up to," she said, sitting across from me. "You tryin' to hit up the club because you know that shit gon' be live for Kane's birthday party. And you know Yolo gone be there."

She caught me but I didn't want to let her ass know that, so I simply shook my head and waved her away.

"Uh huh," she replied, shooting me a smile before looking down at the heels that I'd just kicked off my feet. Them shits hurt like hell. I didn't know how the fuck females walked around in stilettos all day, but I was flat-footed like a muthafucka and I wasn't feeling it.

"Um… put them shoes on and let's go. They not lookin' good for nobody on the damn floor. And learn how to close ya fuckin' legs," she said, pushing my thighs together.

"You should talk, ho," I remarked, laughing as I pushed her away. She pretended to be offended and then rolled her eyes.

"What's goin' on with you and Tank now?"

A smile came to Faviola's face and I already knew what the deal was. She was back feeling that nigga. I don't know what kind of relationship they had and I don't think anyone would be able to figure it out. I guess it worked for them though so what could I say?

"That's still my boo," Faviola replied and then checked in the mirror while applying her lipstick. She turned around and fluffed her curly weave before checking out her backside to make sure her ass looked nice, and then turned to me.

"A'ight! Let's go!"

Shit, I thought as I looked at the heels on the floor and pulled at the short hem of my dress. *What the hell had I been thinking?*

***

When we got to the club, it was already live. Being that I worked there part-time, I didn't have to wait in the long ass line outside and I was thankful for that, because these tight ass heels was not going to last that long. I couldn't wait until I got behind the bar so I could kick them off my damn feet.

"Damn, Sidney! Is that you, baby girl?" my coworker, Mike, asked as I walked in the club and hobbled behind the bar. My feet felt like they were on fire. I rolled my eyes and stuck my tongue out at him as he laughed but, deep down, I felt good about how many men were looking at me. This *never* happened.

"I'm just tryin' somethin' new, but don't get used to it so chill," I told him with a smirk. He nodded his head and then reached over, taking the bottle from out of my hand as I prepared to mix up a drink from a regular.

"Naw, baby, you look too good for this shit tonight. Go on out there and dance or some shit. Give a nigga somethin' to look at," he said and licked his lips.

Looking at him, I wondered if he was referring to himself or to Yolo. Although our lil' fling had been a secret, to the ones who knew me, it was obvious how much I was feeling him. I nodded my head and began to walk out from behind the bar but my nerves were all over the place.

"Go ahead," Mike egged me on once again. "Might as well because he's already lookin' at you."

Sucking in a breath, I looked over to where Mike was nodding his head and locked right into Yolo's eyes. He was sitting next to Kane and Tank, who had Faviola sitting on his lap, and sipping from a Styrofoam cup as he stared directly at me.

"Oh my God," I said, instantly turning into a girl. "What do I do?"

"Damn, that nigga done brought out the chick in you for real. Must be love," Mike laughed, and I swear I wanted to punch him in the face for that shit.

Looking up, I glanced back at Yolo and saw that he was standing up and walking straight towards me, his eyes planted on my face as he moved, paying no attention to anything else. I sucked in another breath and held it before blowing it out slow. I'd known this nigga for years and not once had he ever talked to me in public unless it was on the basketball court. Every moment we had shared other than that had been in private, with just only us. And yeah, it sounds all romantic until you really think about it and understand that it meant he didn't want to be seen in public with me.

Mike pushed a cup of something in my hand and I wasted no time sipping from it. Whatever it was, it was strong as hell and I was every bit grateful because I could use some liquid courage in my life.

"Damn, Sidney, I ain't even kno' it was you," Yolo said as he walked over to me. He was standing close. Real close. But we weren't touching. However, the way he was staring at me had me feeling like it was the onset of some crazy mental foreplay.

"I can't do this shit too, Yolo," I told him with a shrug. "I just think it's stupid. It ain't me."

"It *is* you," he corrected me. Reaching out, he ran his hand over my face, gently. He traced a line from my temple all the way down to under my chin. I dropped my eyes, feeling the passion igniting inside of every piece of my body. It was too much… I could barely stand it.

Yolo lifted my head up with one finger, cupping under my chin, and made me look directly at him. I was in love and there wasn't a damn thing I could do. And he knew it, too. There was no hiding it. Yolo knew that he had me exactly where he wanted me and, until I was able to get this demon of love up off my ass, he always would.

"You did this for me?" he asked, pulling his hand from my face only to run it down the side of my body. He lingered a little longer when he got to my hips and then slid his hand around my waist, pulling me into him.

"Yes."

Wait… what?! No, I did not do this for him. No, no, no!

"You did?" he asked, a boyish grin crossing his face. He bit his lip and I focused on the small 'S' tattoo that he had there. You could barely see it because he kept a little bit of hair right under his lip and it usually covered it up, but I knew about it so I couldn't help but notice it.

When we were teenagers, we had our first fight after he made love to me one night and then showed up to my homegirl's birthday party the next day with another bitch. We fought viciously. He never touched me but I beat the shit out of his ass, to the point that he had no choice but to knock me on my ass to get me off of him. I cried for days and refused to speak to him but I wasn't the only one miserable. He was too. He came back about five days later, showing up at my window in the middle of the night and showed me his new tattoo, the first one he'd ever gotten. It was an "S" for Sidney he told me. And, just like that, he had me back.

Behind my ear, I had a tattoo, also. It was a J for Jace, Yolo's government name. But my younger brother, Jaton, had died after getting shot by a stray bullet when he was twelve, and no one knew Yolo's real name so they assumed it was for Jaton. I never corrected them, so only Yolo knew the truth.

That was the first time Yolo had broken my heart but it wasn't the last. However, none of that shit seemed relevant right now.

"Yeah," I repeated breathlessly, completely overtaken by him.

"Damn," he said, smiling a little as he bent his eyes once more to look me over. He pulled his bottom lip in and sucked on it in a way that sent me plummeting down memory lane, thinking about all the things he used to do with his tongue.

"Why don't you come and chill wit' a nigga?" he asked finally, and my heart skipped a beat.

"For real?" I frowned. This was too much change in one day. I was in heels and a dress, plus, my hair wasn't in a messy ass lopsided ponytail. I was wearing a face full of makeup, Yolo was talking to me in public, and he had invited me to chill with him and his brothers. This was too much. Like *tew* much!

"Yeah, I don't wanna let ya pretty ass out my sight," he smirked, and I took a deep breath, feeling the alcohol starting to really settle in.

Yolo grabbed my hand and started to pull me away and I was just about to go right with him, when something stopped my feet from moving and I frowned. Sensing that I wasn't moving, Yolo turned around and looked at me, crinkling his brows when he saw the look on my face.

"What's up?" he asked.

"What's up is that this is some bullshit!" I spat, snatching my hand from out of his. Yolo's head jerked like he wasn't sure he'd heard me correctly, but it was okay. I had a lot more to say.

"Huh?"

"*This…*" I pointed from him to me, "…is some bullshit! I wasn't good enough for you when I was me, but now you wanna chill with me because I went and got bitched up enough for you!"

Yeah, I said 'bitched up'. I have no idea exactly what I meant but that drink Mike gave me had me on one. I was on my Beyoncé shit, looking fine as hell and making up imaginary words as I pleased.

"Why you trippin', Sidney? A nigga just wanna chill—" Yolo reached out to grab my hand but I snatched away. He clenched his jaw tight and glanced around to see if anyone was watching, which a few people were. I still didn't care.

"Hell naw, Yolo, because I'm sick of your shit! Why did I have to do all this for you to get your shit together? Why couldn't I just be me and you be cool with me being who the fuck I—"

Grabbing me, Yolo pulled me close and crushed his lips against mine before I could say another word. I felt my knees go weak as he pressed his body against mine, dropping his hands until they cradled the fullness of my ass. He forced my lips apart with his tongue and deepened our kiss, making everything around us fade away. When he pulled away, I felt like I was in a daze, totally caught up in the way that he made me feel.

Yeah, I was on my Beyoncé swag but Yolo had just hit me with a 'Bow Down Bitch' move, making my mind switch from telling him to 'take his replaceable ass to the left' all the way to me being 'drunk and dangerously in love'.

"C'mon, baby," Yolo said, once he'd finally pulled away. "Let's just chill for a minute and then we can leave, a'ight?"

"A'ight," I replied, allowing him to take my hand in his and lead me over to where he'd been sitting with his brothers.

This was not going to be good and I knew it. I *fucking* knew it.

He's Not You.

Janelle

Chris: *Hey, you feeling better? Wanna go out tonight?*

Me: *No, I'm still not feeling too good.*

*I*t was a lie. A lie I wasn't even sure why I was telling because I didn't have anything else to do. At the same time, I told it because I didn't want to hang out with Chris. I wanted Luke. Chris was nice and the attraction was there but I was starting not to be able to see myself with him anymore.

Grabbing my phone, I sighed and scrolled until I hit Luke's name in my contact list. I bit my lip, hesitating for only a second before I pressed call.

"Aye, wassup?" Luke answered the phone with an uneasiness in his voice like he was tense. I knew it was probably because I never called him. He always initiated contact.

"Hey, I was just—"

"C'mon, babyyyy, what you doin'? I'm ready for you," a woman said in the background, her tone disgustingly flirty as she begged for his attention.

"Yo, chill! I'm on the phone," Luke replied. I heard the woman make a groaning noise as if she were pouting before a door closed.

"I'm sorry, I didn't know you were busy," I told him, trying to ignore the aching in my chest. Here I was, miserable because I wanted to be with him and he was hanging with some other woman.

"I'm not. I was 'bout to be but… naw, what's up wit' ya, Nell?" he asked just as tears came to my eyes. Why the hell was I about to cry? Why was I being so damn emotional about this? Luke and I had never talked about making anything official. He wasn't my man and I wasn't his girl. I knew this!

"Nothing. I don't know why I called," I said, wiping the tears from my eyes. "I'm about to go to sleep."

"Janelle—"

Closing my eyes, I hung up the phone before he could say another word. I couldn't believe that I actually put myself in that position. I couldn't believe that I was actually falling for him. Grabbing up my things, I headed to my room, ready to just be done with the day. If I could go to sleep, maybe I wouldn't wake up feeling the same way. After changing into my night clothes, I laid in the bed and watched reruns of *Scandal* until I fell asleep, determined not to cry about someone who could never be the one for me.

***

"Oh GOD!" I screamed, jumping up in my bed.

There was a blaring ringing noise in my ears and I awoke startled, only to realize that it was my phone. I'd fallen asleep with my face on top of it and it had scared the shit out of me. Rubbing my eyes, I squinted in the dark at the name on the screen. It was Luke.

"Hello?" I croaked into the phone. In spite of how hurt I'd been only a little bit before, I couldn't ignore the excitement in my chest at being able to hear from him.

"Open the door," was all he said before hanging up.

"Open the..." I frowned as I ran his words through my mind once more before it finally hit me what he was telling me to do.

Standing up, I ignored the fact that I was only wearing some small, thin, lace pajama shorts and a tank top, and took off down the hall and past the living room. Without looking out the peephole, I unlocked all of the locks and snatched the door open, my heart beating wildly in my chest.

As soon as the door came open, my eyes fell on him. He was standing in front of me in all his thuggish glory, loose hair pulled up into a high ponytail, half-braided on one side, black hoodie with a camouflage vest on over it, and black sweatpants with some fresh ass sneakers. He looked at me under his low eyes, before allowing them to run freely over my body, resting for a beat longer on my exposed legs before he came back up to my face.

It was then that I realized I'd been holding my breath and I let it out slowly as I watched him watch me. My panties were soaked and I was throbbing for him. The cool night breeze was making my nipples hard through my tank top... or were they hard because of him? Either way, he noticed it and reached out, pressing down hard on one with his thumb. I sucked in a breath, my eyes grew heavy and I felt my knees get weak.

Without saying a word, Luke scooped me up in his arms and I wrapped my legs around his waist, as he kicked the door closed behind him. He kissed me, our tongues intertwined as our passion grew to enormous amounts, totally enveloping us in our emotions. It was overwhelming how much I wanted him—more than I'd ever wanted anyone. Now I could see why everyone sang his praises and women chanted his name. He was irresistible. And right now, he was mine.

Luke sucked on my tongue as he laid me on the bed, pushing his fingers up my shorts as he ran his hand along my clit, making my whole body quiver. He undressed me before pulling off his own clothing and I watched him, my heart swelling in my chest as my feelings for him grew with every second. I watched as he skillfully placed on a condom before giving me a look that sent chills down my spine, as he licked his lips in anticipation.

But when he leaned down and pushed himself into me, totally feeling me with his girth, I almost came instantly. He felt good to me… *inside* of me. I wanted him to stay in me forever.

"I missed you. I swear I did," he said as he stroked me deep, rendering me speechless for a few seconds. "Ya hear me?"

"Yes," I panted as I caught his stroke, matching it while pulling him close. "I missed you too. SHIT!"

Luke began stroking me harder, more forcefully, jabbing me right to the core and I knew he was about to cum. But I came first, gnashing my teeth and digging my nails into his back, begging for more while also pleading for him to stop. He had my mind totally fucked up in more ways than one.

After we were done, he scooped me into his arms and held me tight, my back pressed against his chest. I started to fall asleep to the rhythm of his heart beating against me, realizing that this was the only place I wanted to be.

I was in love with him. I was in love with a man who was everything I didn't need but everything I wanted all at the same time. Deep down, I knew I'd opened up a can of bullshit that I would have to deal with later on but right then, in this moment, I didn't care.

TO BE CONTINUED!

NOTE FROM PORSCHA STERLING

Thank you for reading!

I seriously love this story and I hope you did too! Don't worry, I never take forever for the next part so you already should know that part 2 will be out VERY SOON! I can't wait to show you what else Janelle, Luke, Carmella, Cree, Sidney & Yolo have in store! But… in part 2, you'll also be able to look further into the lives of some of the others mentioned in this book as well!

I can't tell you too much yet but what I can tell you is that Janelle was right… she definitely opened up a can of ish!

Check out my website to get an overview of the characters mentioned in this installment of the series. I pulled some visuals so you'll know what they kind of look like to me when I'm writing about them. Hope you like what you see! Visit www.porschasterling.com to check them out!

I love to interact with my readers because I APPRECIATE ALL OF YOU! Hit me up!

Please make sure to leave a review! I love reading them!

I would love it if you reach out to me on Facebook, Instagram or Twitter!

Also, join my Facebook group! If you haven't already, text PORSCHA to 25827 to join my text list. Text ROYALTY to 42828 to join our email list and read excerpts and learn about giveaways.

Peace, love & blessings to everyone. I love allllll of you!

Porscha Sterling

MAKE SURE TO LEAVE A REVIEW!

Text PORSCHA to 25827
to keep up with Porscha's latest releases!

To find out more about her, visit www.porschasterling.com

Join our mailing list to get a notification when Leo Sullivan Presents has another release! Text **LEOSULLIVAN** to **22828** to join!

To submit a manuscript for our review, email us at leosullivanpresents@gmail.com